George Henry Wilson

Miscellaneous Poems

George Henry Wilson

Miscellaneous Poems

ISBN/EAN: 9783337205461

Printed in Europe, USA, Canada, Australia, Japan

Cover: Foto ©Andreas Hilbeck / pixelio.de

More available books at **www.hansebooks.com**

MISCELLANEOUS

POEMS

BY

G. H. WILSON.

Ossett:
S. Cockburn & Son, The Borough Printing and Publishing
Works and Offices of the *Ossett Observer*.

—

1896.

PREFACE.

HAVING been asked repeatedly, by my friends, to publish some of my poems in book form, I have at last ventured to do so, but not without some misgivings as to their reception by those who may read them.

Many of these pieces have appeared previously in newspapers, &c., and one of my earliest efforts was published in the *Ossett Observer* in the year 1867.

Some of the shorter poems were written under adverse circumstances, viz., when I was working amid the whirl and busy hum of machinery in the factory twenty-five years ago. Others have been composed during the past few years, in spare moments which have been snatched from a somewhat active commercial life. Most of them have been written specially for young people, and have been printed and presented in pamphlet form to the children in the Sunday Schools of the Ossett district.

I am perfectly aware that the country is almost flooded with books of poems, and that the general reader has not much taste for this class of literature. Yet I hope, notwithstanding the adverse criticism which I know this small volume will receive, that nevertheless it may do some little good to those who peruse its contents.

G. H. WILSON.

Heath House,
    Ossett,
May, 1896.

CONTENTS.

—:o:—

POEMS

BY

GEORGE HENRY WILSON.

MISCELLANEOUS.

LINES WRITTEN ON VISITING THE RUINS OF TINTERN ABBEY.

I stand and gaze upon thy walls, which rise
In all their lofty grandeur toward the skies,
And think of days long passed, when holy men
Thy sacred precincts trod with awe, and when
They chanted forth with low and solemn sound
Their evening hymn, then falling to the ground
Before the altar, crossed themselves, and prayed
With ardent fervent zeal, as there they laid.
But centuries now have fled, and all around
Is hushed and still, while silence reigns profound ;
And, as thy ruined piles I thus behold,
And picture to my mind the days of old,
When in majestic beauty thou didst stand
The pride and admiration of the land,
My soul is overwhelmed—as I here gaze
On thy dismantled towers, decked with the rays
Of yonder setting sun.   But where are now

Those monks of old, I ask, whose solemn vow
Was held so dear, whose holy lives were spent
Within the shadows of thy tenement ?
And from thy walls, the echoing answer comes,
"They sleep, and long have slept in mouldering tombs."
But, though their bodies have become the prey
Of worms, and mingled with the dust they lay,
Yet they shall rise again, even when thou
Hast crumbled into dust and none shall know
The place where thou hast stood.   Yea, they shall rise
And worship in a shrine beyond the skies,
A temple grander far than thou hast been
Or mortal eyes below have ever seen.

ENGLAND'S WELCOME TO STANLEY.

Welcome, Stanley, brave and true ! we hail thee once
        again
To Britain's sea-girt Isles, from Afric's dreary plain ;
The dangers thou hast passed have won thee glorious
        fame,
And England's warmest praise thou now canst justly
        claim.
Our plaudits we would give ; each British heart and
        tongue
Is raised in friendly greeting in one united song.
Thou, bold and gallant hero, hast gained the world's
        renown,
And Britain waits to deck thee with the Victor's crown :
Long mayst thou live, and may God's providence attend
Thee all thy future life, where'er thy steps may bend ;
And may each coming year yet more successful prove
In crowning thy achievements of labour and of love.

THE DEATH OF LORD TENNYSON.

LET England now bewail and mourn the loss
Of one whose honoured name the nation long
Has held so dear, and whose immortal songs
Shall sacred still remain, though he has gone.

And if 'tis true that, when the soul removes
And quits this mortal tenement, it soars
On high, and, freed from all impediments,
Lives on, and far above th' ethereal sky
With God in immortality endures—
Then, even though his mortal flesh decays,
And moulders in the cold and silent tomb,
Yet Tennyson still lives, and will remain
Enshrined within the hearts of those who shall
In future ages read, or sing the lines
Which his poetic soul and lofty mind
Have pictured with artistic skill ; and thus
Shall live again, e'en when his lifeless clay
Has mingled with the ashes of his grave.

O, may the mantle he has worn so long,
But now hath cast aside, without a stain
Or blemish, like Elijah's mantle fall
On some poetic soul, and may its charm
And hidden power unfolded be, and may
Its influence be felt in coming years.

Then peace be to thy dust, oh ! Tennyson—
And joy eternal to thy soul be given ;
No better epitaph could'st thou desire,
Nor could thy loving nation wish thee less.

LINES ON THE BIRTHDAY OF A FRIEND.

NIGH twenty years ago your form so fair
Was clad in childhood's garb. Yet did compare
With some rich casket, where a jewel bright
Has oft been hid, for years, from mortal sight.
But as through changing time your graceful form
More lovely grew, though often by the storm
Of life's dark tempests hid, this sparkling gem
Shone brightly forth, like some rare diadem.
And now, as I behold your face so sweet,
Without a blemish, and in smiles complete—
My soul is moved to poesy and love,
While thus I write my warm esteem to prove.
But ere I close these lines of birthday muse
And lay aside my pen—please to excuse
My lack of language, rightly to express
The feelings which do now my soul possess.
Yet with these thoughts my heartiest wishes blend
In truest friendship, that shall never end.

LINES ON SCANDAL.

THIS is how to begin scandal—
    Someone will say—" I *think* "—
    And that is the first link
In forming the chain of scandal.

Now the next link forged in scandal
    Is saying—" I *believe* "—
    Not meaning to deceive ;
Yet adds to the chain of scandal.

Another link added to scandal—
    Somebody says—" I *know* "—
    Therefore, it must be so ;
Thus strengthening the chain of scandal.

That's not the last link in scandal—
      Another states—" I *saw* "—
      And so on, there you go—
That is the way to forge scandal.

So scandal, with idle chatter
      Began, then on it grew
      Until it seemed quite true—
But to gossips it did not matter.

Did you ever think of the evil
      Which this scandal might do ?
      If so, always be true,
Nor help the wiles of the devil.

MEDITATIONS ON THE DYING YEAR.

DYING are the embers of another fleeting year,
    And soon it will be past and gone for ever ;
How days and weeks and months do quickly disappear,
    And all our old associations sever !

As we look back upon the years now fled away,
    We view, no doubt, with pain, the vows we cherished ;
For all along our pathway trodden day by day
    We find it strewn with resolutions, perished.

God's word declares, " That no one to himself can live,"
    To good or evil all our lives are tending—
And every word, or action, will most surely give
    A blessing or a curse that is unending.

Then help us, Lord, to live, that in the coming year
    We may each moment strive with zeal to render
A good account to Thee, that we may ever share
    Thy blessings and Thy mercies sure and tender.

MUSINGS ON THE DEATH OF THE OLD AND THE BIRTH OF THE NEW YEAR.

RETROSPECTIVE.

THE fleeting moments of the dying year
    Were well nigh spent,
As in my silent room I sat, and there
    With thoughts intent,
I pondered o'er the changes I had seen
    In days now gone.
And, as in panoramic view, the scene
    Went gliding on,
I wondered if the memories of the past
    Would ever be
Forgot.   And then my soul became o'ercast,
    As mournfully
I thought of days misspent, of wasted hours,
    And wished the time,
Gone by, would come again.   That all my powers
    Of manhood's prime
Might then be spent in deeds, and not in words—
    " For blest are they
Who do God's will."   For He His aid affords
    To those who pray.

INTROSPECTIVE.

THE scene is changed—another year appears—
    A vision bright
Hath shed its rays athwart my falling tears—
    Oh! joyous light—
For though I never can recall the past—
    Most hideous dream—
Yet by God's grace, while life on earth shall last
    I can redeem
In coming years each moment as it flies—
    And thus improve
My latent talents—yea, be accounted wise
    By Him above,

Who gives a rich reward for labour done.
    And when on earth
My toils are o'er, and I God's praise have won,
    My native worth
Will then receive its due reward, and I
    A better life
Shall live, in brighter realms beyond the sky,
    Free from all strife.

THE DEATH OF THE DUKE OF CLARENCE
AND AVONDALE.

WEEP, ye sons of England, and deeply now bewail
The loss we have sustained, for our Illustrious Prince,
And future King-elect, is dead! How sad to tell
The mournful tidings ; yet throughout the British Isles
The woeful news has spread, and nations all lament
Our Prince's death. 'Twas but as yesterday, that he
So full of joy and hope was filled, and yet to-day
Grim Death has seized him for his prey, and withered,
    dead
He lies, cut down scarce in the prime of life, and when
The future fraught with pleasure seemed, and happiness
His cup of joy o'erflowed, while British hearts and
    tongues
Were waiting eagerly to greet his wedding day,
And join in mirthful song ; but now, instead of song,
The funeral dirge we hear, and marriage-bells give place
To muffled peal with melancholy sound, and flowers
That would have strewn his bridal path must now be
    used
To deck his shroud, or place upon his youthful grave.

Yet weep not for the dead alone, for those who live
Will need our warmest sympathy — to heal their grief —
That we can ever give ; and one there is, whose heart
Is torn with deepest sorrow, one day Bride-elect,
And then upon the morrow bereft of him she loved —
What wild despair she feels, what pain and anguish tears

Her throbbing breast,—then weep for Her.   And also
        mourn
For our beloved Queen, whose aged and widowed head
Is bowed again with grief, as o'er the silent dead
She bends, and once again her wounded heart is rent
As she remembers Him she loved, who long ago
A victim fell to Death's relentless hand, and passed
Away both honoured and beloved by all the land.

LINES ON THE DEATH OF THE REV. C. H. SPURGEON.

GONE ! Gone ! How sad the loss we have sustained—
Let nations all bewail with helpless grief
The death of one of England's brightest gems,
Whose life with lustre shone, who often cheered
The hearts with sadness filled, and helped to raise
The fallen outcast, from a life of shame
Unto a life of honour and of joy.
        But now, he's dead ! And o'er his silent grave
The widow and the orphan bow their heads
And weep, as only those can weep, who feel
Their benefactor gone—whose hand had helped
Life's burden to remove, and smoothed the cares
From many a weary brow.   And as they stand
And view the tenement, which now contains
His lifeless clay, that death's relentless hand
Has withered almost in the prime of life,
Their bleeding hearts are torn afresh with grief,
While bitter tears bedew the sacred ground.
        Yet in their sorrow, they may find a hope
To banish all their woe, and thus inspire
Their aching throbbing breasts (nor mourn their loss),
For, though his body moulders in the dust,
His soul still lives, and thousands yet will bless
His honoured name.   Yea, many still unborn
Will praise " High Heaven " that Spurgeon ever lived.

LINES WRITTEN ON THE DEATH OF THE MAYOR OF OSSETT, ALD. NETTLETON.

DEATH, the mortal foe of man, again has come,
And with his fierce relentless hand has seized
One in our midst, whose strong and manly form
Foreboded well, and promised in the future
Many days of happiness. How swift the change—
'Twas but as yesterday our worthy Mayor stood
Surrounded by his family, and beloved
By those who knew him best ; his cheerful smiles
Portrayed his genial character, while o'er his face
The hue of health shone forth, nor was there sign
Of " foul disease or sudden dissolution."
But wider still by far, beyond the narrow bounds
Of his own family circle, will the loss
Be felt and mourned.—The Council of the Town
Could ill afford to lose his helpful aid :
For, though he could not boast of cultured tongue
Or eloquence, yet with out-spoken words
And earnest zeal he strove with all his power
To aid the public good, nor feared the frowns
Of those who saw not with him eye to eye,
But steadily pursued till he attained
The object which he sought. And when at last
The town on him conferred, by one consent,
Its highest honour, with quiet dignity
He took the proud position ; and well he filled
The Mayoral chair, nor did he ever swerve
From duty's call, but his attention gave
To help the Borough's weal ; but ere the year
Of office round had sped, his sudden death
A shock of sadness spread and nigh o'erwhelmed
His townsmen's hearts with sorrow and with woe.
And now the tomb contains his lifeless clay,
And o'er his grave his widow bends with grief,
While at her side his son and daughters stand
—Whose hearts are torn—Nor can they realise
At once how great the loss they have sustained :

But often in the future, when they see
The vacant chair, and miss the form they loved,
Their tears will flow afresh, and time alone
Will stem their sorrow's tide and heal their grief.

AN ODE TO THE RIGHT HON. W. E. GLAD-
STONE ON HIS 83RD BIRTHDAY.

GLADSTONE, to thee the Nation now would pay
Its warmest tribute of esteem and love.
Statesman and scholar—thou no compeer hast—
Whose lengthened life has for thy country's weal
Been spent.   Whose hoary head and silvery locks
Give evidence that soon the mighty power
Which thou hast wielded in the past, for good,
Shall cease ; but ere thy work is laid aside
We pray that thou, like others who have steered
The helm of this vast Empire, and whose lives
Were crowned with victory, by Heaven may be
Deck'd with a victor's wreath, and crowned at last.

Though fourscore years and three have passed away
Since thou upon life's stage didst first appear—
And threescore years thy life hath now been spent
In arduous toil, sometimes beneath the smiles
Of men, and sometimes 'neath their frowns, yet still
With true undaunted zeal thy noble life
Is offered as a living sacrifice,
On the altar of thy beloved country.

Oh, may thy closing years successful prove,
In this one last great effort thou dost make
To aid in raising from its low estate
The Nation, which has long by unjust rules
Been crushed, yet whose brave men have keenly fought
Shoulder to shoulder in defence of right.

And ere, most gallant leader, thou shalt quit
The scene, where many a battle thou hast won
In aid of justice, truth and liberty :
Oh, may the flag of freedom wave again
Upon our *Sister Isle*, and equal laws
Be given, that *she* with us in truest bonds
Of union may, by one consent, be joined,
And as *one nation* may we stand or fall.

MARRIAGE OF THE "DUKE OF YORK" AND "PRINCESS MAY."

YE marriage bells, the joyful tidings spread !
　　Peal forth your merry chimes both far and wide ;
For England's future King to-day hath wed
　　The lovely Princess May, his honoured bride.

Let Britain's sea-girt isles their tribute bring
　　In honour of the happy Royal pair,
While loyal subjects make the valleys ring
　　With loud huzzas ! that echo through the air.

Let drum and fife and cymbals now be heard,
　　As youths and maidens dance on village green ;
Let trumpets sound, and hearts be thrilled and stirred
　　To cheer the nuptials of our future Queen.

God bless the noble Duke and fair Princess :
　　May peace and joy attend them all their days,
And may their lives be crowned with happiness,
　　Is now the prayer which joins our festive lays.

TO ROSIE WILSON ON HER TENTH BIRTHDAY.
AUGUST 31st, 1892.

So you are ten years old this birthday,
　　And you say your name is Rose !
Why, you are growing quite a lady,
　　And *you think so, I suppose ?*

Yes, you have had as many birthdays
  As there are fingers on your hands—
Please accept my heartiest wishes :
  And may the bright and golden bands
Which unite your life unto others
  Be strong, and unsevered remain—
And may all your life in the future
  Be *as sunshine after the rain.*

And when your life here shall be ended
  May you live in that happier place
Where no birthdays are ever recorded
  And no years can your beauty deface.

THE BOY AND THE PARSON.

A BRIGHT little boy was playing one day,
In a village street 'mong the mud and clay,
When a Parson happened to pass that way.
Said he to the boy—" What is it you're making ?"
For he saw that a model he was shaping
From dirt in the gutter that he was scraping.

The boy looked up, and paused for awhile,
Then, nodding his head, he said with a smile,
" I'm making a church, and this is the aisle,
" And there are the pews—the people as well—
" And that is the steeple—this is the bell—
" Here is the pulpit—What more can I tell ?"

" But where is the Parson ?"—he said to the lad ;
The urchin replied, with face not quite sad,
" There's not enough clay round here to be had."
The Parson then turned, and shaking his head,
Away he did go—his face blushing red—
Repeating the words the boy had just said.

ONLY.

It was only a little sunbeam,
  That shone with its feeble ray,
Through a window up in a garret
  Where a child in suffering lay ;
Yet, though sick and sad and weary,
  It made her heart feel aglow—
As she thought of Him, who so kindly
  His goodness and mercies bestow.

It was only a tiny flower
  That grew on the village green,
And was plucked by a little maiden—
  Though many had passed it unseen—
Yet it cheered the heart of her brother,
  A poor, weak and helpless lad—
For to him 'twas a priceless treasure,
  And made him feel happy and glad.

It was only a kind word spoken
  To one who was filled with grief
And whose tears were silently flowing,
  Yet it brought a smile of relief.
Then let us these trifles remember,
  Nor think them too mean to employ—
For kind words—like flowers and sunbeams
  Will often bring gladness and joy.

A LETTER TO MY CHILDREN AT SCHOOL.

Dear Lily and Rosie, pray list to my rhyme—
Now, as I am writing, I hear the bells chime,
The bright sun is shining, and Spring-tide is here,
In garden and meadow sweet flowers appear.

The primrose and violet, their rich fragrance shed,
The daffodil gracefully hangs down its head—
The daisies are kissing the dewdrops of morn,
Which sparkle like jewels their crowns to adorn.

The trees in the orchard have burst from the tomb
Of winter's strong fetters, and clad in their bloom
Are scenting the air—while the humming of bees
Is wafting like music, and floats on the breeze.

The skylark is mounting aloft in the air,
And from its throat warbles its song sweet and clear,
While the thrush in yon tree sings aloud to its mate,
As she sits by her nest, and for him doth wait.

And you, my dear children, a lesson thus learn,
As daily in nature God's works you discern ;
Be cheerful and happy, contented and free—
Then fairer than flowers in Spring-tide you'll be.

THE MINERS' LOCK-OUT, 1893.

THE fight 'twixt Capital and Labor
  Is waging throughout the land,
And great is the want and suffering
  Which is felt on every hand.

Many children for bread are crying,
  But the shelf at home is bare ;
Thin faces are pinched with hunger
  And wan with want and despair.

Mothers, too, with hearts full of anguish,
  Are stricken with grief and woe ;
And call for our help in their struggle—
  Oh, who to their aid will go ?

Will some kind hearted men and women
  From their store of plenty send—
To save them from want and starvation,
  And prove to suffering a friend?

Let employers of labor consider
  The just demands of the men—
Let employed too listen to reason—
  Their passions curb and restrain.

Each workman of his hire is worthy—
Is a truth which none deny ;
And "fair play "—'tis said—"is a jewel "—
While cheating we all decry.

Then why shouldn't " Capital and Labor "
Join hand in hand, to destroy
The evils of strikes and lock-outs—
And displace misery with joy?

A LETTER.

DEAR Lily and Rosie, as I take up my pen
Please excuse me if prosey ; for now and again
I fancy my letters are not so attractive
To children whose minds are so buoyant and active.

And, first, I would write of the state of the weather
Which at present is dull, and not altogether
Just what we would like it—Alas ! it is raining—
You see I still grumble, and oft am complaining.

Once more, I'm reminded that Xmas is nearing,
When faces so sad will be made bright and cheering,
For good *Santa Claus* will, no doubt, give them pleasure
By filling their stockings with gifts they will treasure.

And you, I imagine, have fondly been dreaming
Of that festive season, till your eyes bright and beaming
Have sparkled and shone like the dewdrops of morning,
And now sweetest smiles are your faces adorning.

Then, hurrah ! for the time of beef and plum pudding,
When roast geese and turkeys the tables are studding.
And may peace and plenty be yours, now and ever,
Is the wish of the writer, your loving father.

A LETTER.

DEAR Lily, I now take my pen,
  To write these lines to you :
And, as the clock is striking ten,
  My words must be but few.

I hope you're very well in health,
  Although 'tis wintry weather—
For health is better far than wealth,
  Though both go well together.

How swiftly time is speeding on,
  Though perhaps to you 't seems drear ;
A few more weeks will soon be gone,
  And Christmas will be here.

Please give my love to darling Rose,
  And kiss her for me too—
She'll laugh and shout I do suppose,
  And make a lot to do.

Ma ! says she is a charmer, O,
  And growing very big—
" So she will not be frightened, No !
  Not even by a pig."

But now I must conclude my rhyme,
  And hurry off to bed,
'Tis eleven o'clock—I hear it chime—
  And weary is my head.

Yet, ere my pen I now lay down,
  Permit me thus to sign—
Yours very truly—George Wilson—
  This should be the last line.

P.S.—Your Ma and Freddy also send
    Their love to you in rhyme—
  And forward look, with you, to spend
    A happy Christmas time.

"THE CRY OF ARMENIA."

How long, O Lord, shall persecution reign
And cruel tyrants crush beneath their feet
Armenia's Sons?   Will nations all refuse
To lend a listening ear?   And shall they cry
For help in vain?   Behold them in their deep
And abject misery, crushed to the earth
By fiends in human form, whose reeking swords
Are steeped, e'en to the hilt, in blood of slain.

For ages past those faithful Christians
Have suffered woes untold.   The Turkish hordes
Have often been let loose upon them, and
Their wives and daughters have been ravished by
Those hellish fiends.   Then who will volunteer
To help them?   For 'tis not enough that we
As Englishmen should seek to mitigate
Their woes by saving from starvation's verge.

What we, as Britain's sons, should now demand,
E'en by our swords and guns, is this—To end
For aye the Sultan's reign.   Too long " the Powers
That be" have bolstered up that kingdom, which
Is rotten to the core, and which should now
By our united efforts be o'erthrown.

Then with one loud and soul-enthrilling cry
Let England now declare, that tyranny
Shall end, and freedom thus be given to brave
Armenia's sons.   So will the sympathy
And gratitude of all the world be earned.

CHRISTMAS STORIES

and other pieces written specially
for Young People.

WILLIE CHESTER,
THE LITTLE MATCH-SELLER.

It was on the eve of Christmas—
    Yes, merry Christmas time ;
When peace, joy and mirth, and goodwill on earth
    Rang out in every chime.

And the night was cold and stormy,
    The snow fell thick and fast,
As with hurried feet, through the busy street,
    The crowds were moving past.

Some faces looked sad and weary,
    As they walked with haste along ;
And some, with a smile, would pause for awhile,
    To gaze on the busy throng.

Some were clad in tattered garments,
    And seemed half starved with cold ;
While others were dressed in robes of the best,
    Trim'd with fur, rich to behold.

And they all seemed very eager,
    Some nice present to possess ;
The rich, with their gold, would treasures unfold,
    The poor were content with less.

But in the hurry and bustle
  None heeded the plaintive cry
Of a little lad, who, with face so sad,
  Called out to the passers-by,

" Who will buy a box of waxlights—
  " A penny a box ?" he said ;
And he shivered with cold, for his garments were old,
  While bare and wet was his head.

He was only young and feeble,
  His voice you could scarcely hear ;
Yet he tried to sell, for he knew quite well
  The cupboard at home was bare.

And mother, he knew, was waiting,
  Yes, waiting now to receive
The pence from her boy, so that she might buy
  Some food, on that Christmas eve.

For, though she was poor and helpless,
  Her heart was loving and kind,
And her darling boy was her pride and joy,
  And round him her heart entwined.

They had not always been needy—
  No, brighter days they had seen ;
But sorrow and woe, with their cruel blow,
  To darken their home had been.

'Twas only five years that winter—
  Yes, 'twas just five years ago—
A man had been found, laid dead on the ground,
  And almost covered with snow.

That man was poor Willie's father,
  And drink had been his curse ;
Though often he tried his weakness to hide,
  He went from bad to worse.

Yet he loved his boy when sober,
    He was fond of mother too ;
And none more inclined to be gentle and kind,
    Or ever a heart more true.

But, alas ! his love for liquor
    Grew stronger, till at last
Both position of trust and honour he lost,
    Ere many years had passed.

Thus his home was brought to ruin ;
    His wife and only child,
Through his sad disgrace, had the world to face,
    Which drove him nearly wild.

Then he sought to hide his sorrow,
    And drown his shame in beer ;
Till that winter's night, in an awful plight,
    He ended his sad career.

And when they had found his body,
    Frozen to death in the snow,
None were left to mourn, save mother and son,
    That day, just five years ago.

Since then the widow had struggled
    Herself and boy to maintain ;
And often she found, as the years rolled round,
    It was hard their bread to win.

But as little Willie grew older,
    Though only a tiny dot,
He often would cheer his mother so dear,
    And help to lighten her lot.

And that was why he sold matches,
    On that stormy winter's night ;
And as he stood there, with blue eyes so fair,
    And gazed on the busy sight,

He wished he was a bit older,
    That he might more useful be ;
Then, with tears in his eyes, he heaved a big sigh,
    As he called out mournfully

To a gentleman who was passing,
    A stranger, with long dark locks—
" Do buy a box, please, do, sir, if you please,
    " Only a penny a box !"

The man he addressed stopped quickly,
    And turned to look at the lad ;
Then he, at a glance, saw here was a chance
    To cheer a heart that was sad,

His own heart was full of kindness,
    For he remembered so well,
How, long years ago, he stood in the snow,
    Trying his matches to sell.

And so he said unto Willie—
    " Why stand you here in the snow ?"
And Willie replied—" Since my father died,
    My mother is poor, you know :

" That is the reason I'm here, sir,
    Do buy a box, if you please ;
They're only a penny, I haven't got many "—
    And he shook in the cold breeze.

Then love filled the heart of the stranger,
    While, tears flowing from his eyes,
To Willie he said, as he raised his head,
    And looked up with surprise,

" What will you take for the lot, lad ?
    Come, tell me now, my boy"—
Then poor Willie gazed, and stood quite amazed,
    His face lit up with joy.

" You can have them all for sixpence"—
    At this, the stranger smiled,
As a piece of gold, from a purse quite old,
    He took, and gave to the child,

Saying, " Never mind the change, boy,
    You may keep it all "—he said ;
" But tell me your name, you need not shame,
    Is it Tom, or Dick, or Fred ?"

" My name, sir, is Willie Chester"—
    " Chester !" the man then replied—
" Yes, sir," Willie said, as he raised his head,
    And his eyes he opened wide.

For he wondered at the question
    Which the stranger asked of him ;
And again, with surprise, he saw that the eyes
    Of the man with tears were dim.

" What was the name of your father ?"
    Again the gentleman said—
" John Chester, sir "—Then, a sigh as of pain
    He heaved, and hung down his head.

Once more, the man fairly started !
    " Could it be ! " Was this the boy
Of his brother John ?" And he looked upon
    The face of the lad with joy,

       *   *   *   *

Now the stranger's name was Chester,
    But nigh twenty years ago
He had left his home, o'er the world to roam,
    Resolving that he would go

And seek for fame and for fortune ;
    So he left his native shore,
And sailed o'er the main, his fortune to gain,
    As many had done before.

And for many years he had struggled,
  Far away in regions wild ;
But, with heart and will, he toiled on, until
  Fortune upon him had smiled.

    *   *   *   *

Now, when from home he departed,
  He left his mother in pain ;
A brother also, who said—" Do not go ;
  I pray you, Bill, to remain

At home, with me and dear mother ;
  Don't leave us here all alone"—
But he heeded not, though sad was their lot :
  " Good-bye," he said, and was gone.

Yes, gone, and left them to struggle,
  With their lot, so dark and sad ;
And for many long years his mother, in tears,
  Did mourn for her wandering lad.

At last she died midst her sorrows,
  And John, her darling son,
Of mother bereft, was all that was left,
  Over her grave to mourn,

    *   *   *   *

Thus years rolled on, and John Chester
  To manhood's prime had arrived ;
Then he wooed and wed, and for years he led
  A sober life, and he strived

To make it a life of goodness—
  While fortune upon him smiled ;
And great was his joy, when a darling boy,
  Their first and their only child,

Was laid on his wife's dear bosom :
  No happier twain could there be ;
And sometimes he said, as he stroked his head—
  " I wish my brother could see

" His dear little charming nephew—
  " I wonder where Bill is now ?"—
But he never heard, not even a word
  Of him, who long years ago

Had sailed o'er the bounding ocean—
  " Oh ! could he be living still,
And would he return ?" How his heart did burn,
  For he loved his brother Bill.

✳   *   ✳   *

But as time passed on, John Chester
  Was tempted to go astray,
And very soon found that the treacherous ground
  From under his feet gave way.

And soon his evil companions,
  From whom he once did shrink,
Dragged him down to shame, and his honoured name
  Was lost through the love of drink.

And the rest of this sad story
  To you is already known ;
How at last a slave, in a drunkard's grave,
  He reaped the seed he had sown.

✳   *   ✳   *

Now, all this time William Chester
  Worked on with might and main ;
Yet he often tried his sorrows to hide,
  And longed for home again.

For though he had prospered greatly,
  Yet he could not happy be ;
So resolved one day no longer to stay
  In that land beyond the sea.

Then at last he sold his business,
  His houses and lands as well ;
And a ship came round, that was homeward bound,
  So he bade his friends farewell.

And just on the eve of Christmas
  Arrived at his native town ;
For only that day he'd sailed in the bay,
  In a vessel called " Renown."

And as he walked through the city,
  The streets of which were filled
With an eager throng—as he pressed along
  He heard a voice, that thrilled

Him through and through with compassion :
  But little did he know
That the voice he heard, which his soul had stirred,
  Through the thick falling snow,

Was the voice of his own nephew,
  Out in the cold, cold, street,
Who was standing there, with his head quite bare
  And nothing on his feet.

But when he had heard the story—
  He said to Willie—" Come,
" Let me take your hand (you can hardly stand),
  " And show me to your home.

" For I am your uncle, darling,
  " I've just come home from sea"—
Then, after awhile, he said with a smile—
  " What have you got for tea ?"

"I'm afraid," said little Willie,
  "We have not got any, sir;
"But with all this cash we'll soon cut a dash,
  "And mother will make a stir.

"I'm so glad that you have come, sir,
  "And mother will be too;
"For she prayed to-day, that God, in His way,
  "Would prove His promise true."

"Thank God; He has heard her prayers!"
  His uncle then replied—
"And now, Willie dear, we will gladly share
  "A happy Christmastide."

And so it was, on the morrow,
  Just at the break of day;
As the bells did ring, and the waits did sing
  Their merry roundelay,

They joined in the happy chorus,
  As tears of joy they shed;
And merry were they, on that Christmas Day,
  For sorrow all had fled.

LITTLE TIM.

It was on Christmas Eve, a many years ago:
The wind was biting cold, and silent fell the snow;
And through the busy streets the crowds were hurrying
    fast.
They quickly moved along to escape the wintry blast,
But many paused awhile, with eager eyes to gaze
Upon the busy scene, for the windows all ablaze
Were garlanded with mistletoe and holly green,
Also fruits and flowers as fine as e'er were seen.

The school had closed, and children tripp'd with glee
As homeward they now ran, so bright and merrily;
But they, too, now have stopped, and stand with
    wondering eyes,
To view the tempting piles, and shout with glad surprise.
"Come, come, young folks!" a voice rings out quite near;
"I really cannot do with children standing here;
"You are blocking up the way, and people cannot see;
"Take these," the shopman said, "and run off home to
    tea."
And, as he spoke, his hands he then did fill
With nuts, and tossed them in their midst, until
The children fairly shouted with delight;
And he, good-natured, smiled to see the sight.

Now, very soon the nuts were gathered up,
And on their way did run the merry troop.
But one there was, a tiny little lad,
Who slowly moved away, with face quite sad,
For in the scramble this little boy had not
Successful been, and so no nuts had got.
The shopman had seen this as he stood by,
And so he called out, "Tim, what makes you cry
"My little chap? Come tell me now," said he.
So Tim replied, "I did not get a nut, you see."
Now Mr. King felt sorry for the boy—
For he remembered one, his pride and joy,
A little son about the age of Tim;
And, as he thought, it made his eyes grow dim
With tears—for Willy, his own darling lad,
Was warmly dressed, while Tim was thinly clad.
Perhaps it was this thought that made him kind
And with compassion filled his heart and mind.
"Come here," he said, "and I'll make up to you
"For losing those few nuts"; and without more ado
He brought a nice rich orange, fine and large,
And placed it in Tim's hand without a charge.
"Oh! thank you," said the boy, with great delight
As o'er his face there shone a joyous light.

[Now little Tim a drunken father had,
And that was why he often looked so sad ;
For many times the cupboard had been bare,
While other boys had plenty and to spare.]

"Have you got your Christmas goose?" he asked of him.
"No, sir, I guess we ain't," said little Tim ;
"They cost too much." And then his eyes he raised
With wistful look, as on the birds he gazed.
"I'll tell you where your Christmas goose is," said he.
"Where? oh, tell me," Tim said quite eagerly.
"Why, at the liquor store, just down the way,
"Where many things besides are stowed away.
"Now go and tell your father what I've said,
"For he knows why you often want for bread."
"I'll go and tell him now," replied the boy ;
And off he ran, his heart quite filled with joy.
Nor did he stop until he reached the place
He called his home, and with a beaming face
That shone quite radiant with delight he said,
"Oh! mother! mother!" And running to the bed
On which a thin and pale-faced woman lay,
With nothing but a blanket, old and grey,
To shield her from the cold and wintry blast.
"Where is father?" said little Tim at last :
His mother pointed to a corner, where
A man in drunken slumber, lying there
Apparently unconscious of it all,
Nor caring what to him there might befall.
"Oh! I must wake him now," exclaimed the lad,
"For I've some news that's sure to make him glad."
"No ; You must not wake him," the mother cried.
Then, as she spoke, she drew Tim to her side,
And asked, "Why do you wish to wake him, dear?"
For oft the lad had stood, in dread and fear
Of father's anger ; but now all fear had gone
As he replied, "Just wait till I have done ;
"I want to tell my father where to go
"To get our Christmas dinner, don't you know?"
"Where is it, dear?" his mother asked of Tim,

As with surprise she shook her head at him.
" Why, at the liquor store," the shopman said ;
" It's true, and so you need not shake your head.
" He told me I might tell my father so.
" Oh ! let me wake him ; then I'm sure he'll go."
At last the mother saw how that the boy
Believed the shopman's words, and to destroy
His happiness she found it very hard.
So, looking at her boy with great and fond regard,
" Tim," she said gently, stroking the dark head
That lay beside her own upon the bed ;
" Do you not know what Mr. King did mean ?
" Here, nestle close to me, and let me screen
" You from the bitter cold, and I will tell
" You what the words have meant, for I know well.
" Now, this is what the shopman really meant :
" Your father at the store has often spent
" His hard-earned money, that would now provide
" A Christmas goose and many things beside."
" Oh ! then, there is no dinner after all
" For us !" said Tim, as from his eyes did fall
Such bitter tears, and silently they flowed,
As on his mother's breast his head he bowed.
The mother for awhile said nothing to the boy,
But kissing him so tenderly, her pride and joy,
She presently the question asked of him,
" Where did you get that nice sweet orange, Tim ?"
At this he rose, and very soon he dried
The tears from off his face ; and then he cried,
" Why Mr. King gave it to me, you know ;
" Oh ! Is it not a beauty, quite fit for any show ?
" We'll keep it for to-morrow, mother dear ;
" And see, I'll hide it in the blanket here."
" Now tell me, Tim, what you have learnt to-day
" At school," his mother said, that she might keep away
His disappointment ; and then Tim replied,
" The teacher spoke of merry Christmas tide,
" And how we should be thankful for our home,
" For many children have no shelter from the storm.
" And then she said that we had parents too ;

" And, mother, I am glad that I have you ;
" But, do you know, I sometimes think that we,—
"(If father were away) might happier be ?
" Hush, Tim my child ; you never more must say
" Such words again, for once there was a day
" When father was both good and kind to me ;
" And perhaps some day he will his error see ;
" So we must love him still, and ever try
" To win him from the paths of misery."

At length she saw that he, whom they supposed
Asleep in drunken stupor, was aroused.
And jumping from the bed on which he lay
He rushed out of the room ; and then away
Into the gathering darkness, on he went
Not caring where the next few hours he spent.

Now, all the time since Tim had first arrived
At home, his father merely had contrived
To affect a drunken slumber, and had heard
Each word that had been said, and so he feared
To think upon the past, for well he knew
That every word of Mr. King's was true.
For only just five years ago John Bell
Had every comfort home could give, as well
As happy wife and child, for whom his love
And pride so constantly did prove
Him worthy of respect by all around.
But, oh ! what was he now ? Why now he found
Himself a poor despised drunkard, the curse
Of all who knew him ; and what by far was worse
Than all, the wife whom once he loved was laid
Upon a bed of suffering he himself had made ;
And Tim, his only child, had wished him gone—
Oh ! was it strange, that as he stumbled on—
On through the darkness, trying now in vain
To escape a guilty conscience, for the pain
Was more than he could bear—at last he found
Himself beside the river's edge, and round
He looked, to see if any one was near :

What better could he do than now and here
To drown himself? for right full well he knew
The words that his own boy had said were true—
" We would be happier without father."   So
He resolved at once, 'twas best that he should go
And plunge into the river running by,
Thus ending, once for all, his agony.

'Twas then he thought he heard a voice quite near :
Was it an angel whispering in his ear?
" No ; be a man, and not a coward base,
" For you may rise by trusting in God's grace.
" Do not destroy your life, but try again
" To win the love you've lost, and you may then
" Successful be in trying to restore
" The happiness which you possessed of yore."
And, as he thought, a longing o'er him came
To break his shackles and his life reclaim ;
But could he do it? Well, he could but try ;
And down he knelt, and with agonizing cry
These words he prayed, " God helping me, I will ;"
And, rising to his feet, he felt a thrill
Of joy! And now resolved, his steps he bent,
And to his old employer's house he went.

Now Mr. Leslie had often tried to win
And save him from the downward course of sin.
So great was his surprise to see again
The man who oft had caused him grief and pain.
Could it be true, that he had come at last
Resolved to break the chains that held him fast ?
And, with a prayer that this the case might be,
A welcome hand he gave both warm and free ;
" Come in out of the cold," he said to John :
And, into his warm room he drew him on,
Saying, " What can I do for you my man ?
" Tell me, and I will help you if I can."
John answered, " Sir, I have resolved at last
" Strong drink to shun, and so redeem the past.
" A favor I would ask of you, kind friend,

"Oh! give me back my work, and I will spend
"My future life, so that it may atone
"For wrongs, that I my wife and child have done."
"With all my heart," his master then replied,
And as he spoke he drew John to his side
And asked him, "Will you sign the pledge for me?"
"Yes, sir, I want to," he said quite eagerly;
And with a firm resolve, though trembling hand,
He signed his name, and joined the Temperance Band.
And when he rose to go, his master then did say,
"To show my trust in you, I now intend to pay
"A week's wage in advance, that you may buy
"The comforts that you need; and now good-bye,
"And may you have a happy Christmas Day,"
Then John, with a glad heart, did haste away,

    ✳   ✳   ✳   ✳   ✳   ✳   ✳   ✳   ✳

About an hour had quickly passed away,
When homeward he returned, where his wife lay
With Tim curled up beside her fast asleep,
While she, half dreading, still her watch did keep.
But when she now beheld her husband dear,
Whose arms were laden full with Christmas cheer,
She saw at once a change had taken place,
For a new light was beaming o'er his face;
Just then, Tim woke, and when he saw the sight,
In ecstacy he fairly shouted with delight,
"Oh! father, I am so glad that you have got
"Our Christmas dinner; and look, oh! what a lot
"You've brought; now shan't we have a jolly treat,
"Why no one ever saw such piles of meat!"

And so it was, while purest love held sway,
They thus did spend a happy Christmas day,

Now for a time John found it hard to free
Himself; but soon he gained the victory,
And henceforth led a new and better life,
For home was free from sorrow and from strife.

And though Tim never knew what made the change
In father, and he sometimes thought it strange
To see him now, so loving and so kind,
And often he would ponder in his mind
Of all the days gone by, and once he said
Unto his mother, as with uplifted head
He looked into her face, now free from pain,
" I love my father, for he's won my heart again."

BILLY AND JACKY, THE TWO ORPHANS.

'TWAS Christmas, happy Christmas-time,
  You could feel it in the air ;
The bells rang out a merry chime,
  And joy seemed everywhere.
The hurrying, jostling crowds were bent
  On errands of goodwill,
As through the busy streets they went,
  Their missions to fulfil.

Old gentlemen, in big fur-coats,
  Were tramping through the snow ;
Their pockets bulging out, quite full—
  Their faces all aglow.
And children, too, went trotting on,
  With little bundles neat ;
Their faces lit with pleasant smiles,
  They ran with merry feet.

But here and there, among the throng
  Of people gaily dressed,
Were those who slowly moved along,
  As through the crowd they pressed ;
And sometimes they would stop and gaze,
  With eager, wistful eye,
Into the windows, all ablaze,
  And then would heave a sigh,
As anxiously they thought of home,
  Of loved ones waiting there,

No doubt expecting to receive
  Of Christmas gifts a share.
And as they held, in their cold hands,
  A purse, both worn and thin,
They pondered how they best could spend
  The hard-earned pence within.

And also rough, good-natured men
  Went jostling through the crowd ;
With hands thrust in their pockets deep,
  They ask, with voices loud,
The prices of the pretty trees
  Which on the pavement lay.
And after buying all they need,
  They proudly march away,
Thinking, no doubt, the coming morn
  Would bring a glad surprise
To many little prattling ones,
  Soon as they op'ed their eyes.

Now all who formed this busy throng
  Were bent so eagerly
Upon their errands of good-will,
  That they had failed to see
Two tiny, half-starved urchins, who,
  In rags and tatters clad,
Stood shivering in the blinding snow,
  With faces worn and sad.
They had no shoes or stockings on ;
  Their feet were blue with cold ;
And in their hands they tightly held
  Their papers, still unsold.
And no one seemed to heed the boys,
  Or listen to their cry ;
Too busy e'en to cast a look,
  They quickly passed them by.
The younger, a mere child of seven,
  With large dark eyes, portrayed
That want had almost done its work,
  And on his form had laid

Its blighting and relentless hand ;
  For every now and then
He coughed—a sharp, dry cough it was,
  That seemed to cause him pain.

The clock in the cathedral tower
  Had now begun to chime ;
Three papers only sold as yet,
  And half-past four the time.
And little Jack now cried with cold,
  So begged that Bill would find
Some place more sheltered from the storm,
  And from the cutting wind.

Billy agreed, and off they ran,
  As fast as they could go,
Unto a well-known empty shed,
  T" escape the driving snow.
And then they close together crept,
  As close as they could be ;
And as the wind blew through the chinks,
  Jack questioned, wistfully—
" Bill, do you think there's wind in heaven,
  " Where mother's gone to dwell?"
And Bill replied, " I reckon not,
  " For I remember well
" She told me all was nice up there,
  " No storms of wind and rain ;
" No winter's snow, no biting cold,
  " Or cough that gives us pain."
Jack shivered, and then asked again—
  " Do all have Christmas there ?
" And have they all nice things to eat,
  " Both plenty and to spare ?"
" Yes ! Oh, yes !" Bill was sure of that,
  And so at once he said—
" There's pies, and cakes, and candy too."
  At this Jack raised his head,
And with his eyes, now opened wide,
  He then with joy did cry—

" I wish, Bill, I could go there now,"
  And gave a long, long sigh.
At this Bill placed his arm around
  His brother's neck, and said,
" Perhaps, Jack, you will go, some day,"
  And then he turned his head
And drew his sleeve across his eyes,
  To hide the falling tears :
For, although only nine years old,
  Brave was he for his years.
And having dashed the tears away,
  To ease his brother's mind,
He rose, and took him by the hand,
  Saying, " We will try to find
" The place called heaven, where mother went."
  And then they pushed their way
On through the crowded, busy streets,
  Where all was bright and gay.

Now Bill could well remember still
  The way the waggon went,
Which bore their mother to the grave ;
  And so his steps he bent
Right on, unmindful of the cold,
  On through the darkening night,
They left the city far behind,
  Which soon was lost to sight.
And on they trudged until the snow
  Grew deep and deeper still,
For there it was not trampled down.
  Yet on they journeyed till
At length they both grew tired and faint,
  And trembled with the cold.
So Bill, at last, said—" Let's go back,"
  And as he spoke there tolled
The city bell, which now struck nine,
  Far in the distant tower.
" I guess we can't get there to-night,
  " For hark, how late the hour ! "

Then Jacky coughed again, but still
  With tearful eyes, said he,
" No, no, Bill, let's go on again,
  " For, perhaps, we soon shall see
" The place called heaven, where mother lives ;
  " It can't be far away,
" And maybe we shall spend with her
  " To-morrow, Christmas Day."

Then on again they side by side
  Tramp through the drifting snow,
With none to cheer and none to guide,
  Alone, alone they go.
Alone ! Ah ! no, for there was One,
  A Friend, who's always nigh ;
Whose ears are ever opened wide
  To hear the Orphan's cry.

At last Jack said, " I am so tired,
  " My eyes won't open keep,
" Let's lay down here upon the snow—
  " I want to fall asleep."
Bill shivered as he said, " No, Jack,
  " You must not lay down here,
" And look, I see such a big light,
  " Perhaps we're nearly there ;
" At any rate, we'll ask the way,
  " Most likely they will know."
So Jack again now started up,
  And onward they did go.

Now very soon they stood before
  A mansion large and fine,
With windows all aglow with light,
  That on the snow did shine ;
The curtains were drawn up, and so
  Bill took a peep into
A room in which a lady sat
  With lots of children too.

And in the room a Christmas tree
  Was decked quite full with toys,
And these the lady shared among
  The little girls and boys.

Now Bill had never seen before
  Such lots of things, you know,
So was it any wonder he
  Forgot the cold and snow,
And for at least five minutes gazed
  Upon the dazzling scene ?
At last he whispered, " Jack, come here,
  " For this is heaven, I ween."
No answer came, and looking round
  He saw that Jack was laid
Upon a heap of drifted snow ;
  And so again he said—
" Come, Jacky, boy, wake up, wake up,
  " We've got to heaven, my dear !
" And I am going inside to see
  " If mother's waiting here."
But still no answer came from Jack ;
  And Billy tried in vain
To shake him from the fatal sleep,
  And make him speak again.

At last he crept up to the door,
  And rang the bell with fear,
On which a tall man, in fine clothes,
  Did quickly then appear.
" Please, sir," said Bill, " I want to know
  " If mother is inside ?
" And, please, sir, is this place called heaven ?"
  At which the man replied,
In tones quite stern,—" What do you want ?"
  Thinking, no doubt, that Bill
Was only wanting food to eat ;
  And so, with voice quite shrill,
" You cannot come in here," he said,
  " But to the kitchen go,

" For beggars never are allowed
  " To come this way."   And so
He turned away, about to shut
  The door in Billy's face,
When, just in time, the lady came
  And asked to hear the case ;
And with a little questioning,
  She soon Bill's troubles knew ;
So, calling to her husband, said,
  " Go, bring his brother, too."
But little did they think that Jack,
  Now lying in the cold,
Would spend to-morrow's Christmas Day
  Within the Saviour's fold.

Good Mr. Sempton soon returned,
  With Jacky on his arm ;
But, as he laid him on the couch,
  He said, with some alarm,
" I am afraid this little man
  " Is past all human aid ;
" But we must try to save his life."
  And so he quickly said,
" Tell John to harness ' Bob ' at once,
  "And I with him will go
" To fetch the doctor right away.
  "And mother, you will know
"Just what to do till we return ;
  " We shan't be long, my dear."
So, kissing her, he left the room,
  And rushed away in fear.

Now for a time Bill did not know
  What Mr. Sempton meant,
But their sad faces troubled him,
  As o'er poor Jack he bent ;
And, giving him a gentle pull,
  He whispered in his ear—
" I say, we've got to heaven, you know,
  "Come, wake up, Jacky dear."

Christmas-eve had well-nigh gone,
  And soon the bells would ring
In honour of the Saviour's birth,
  Who did glad tidings bring !
And in the silent room they watched,
  With anxious eyes, now bent
Upon the couch where Jacky lay—
  Their faces all intent,
Waiting to catch the faintest sign
  Of his returning life.
At last the doctor said, " I fear
  " 'Twill end his mortal strife."
And as he spoke he turned away,
  The falling tears to hide,
And thought of one, a darling child,
  Who long ago had died.
He also thought of those at home
  Sleeping so peacefully,
And from his heart there rose a prayer
  That they might happy be.

At last a little sigh is heard,
  Then quick his tears he dried,
And turning to the couch, he saw
  Jack's eyes were open wide.
And, gazing round the dazzling room,
  A smile his face did fill
As faintly he now whispered, " Heaven !
  But where is Ma and Bill ?"

Now Bill had been well fed and dressed,
  So he had begged to stay
Just in a corner of the room
  Where little Jacky lay.
So now he from the corner stole,
  And with a tearful face
He said to Jack, " Ma is not here,
  " And this is not the place
" Where mother lives."   And as he spoke,
  O'er Jacky's face there passed

A cloud of sorrow and distress,
　　That now his brow o'ercast.

But there in the dim light, before
　　The dawn of Christmas Day,
The story old was once more told
　　About the heavenly way.
And, as they spoke of Christ and heaven,
　　Jack asked in feeble tone,
" Is mother waiting for me there ?
　　"And shall I see her soon ?"
" Yes, dear," the answer came ; and then
　　He for awhile was still,
But soon he whispered, " Oh ! I wish
　　" I could go now, with Bill."
" O ! we'll take care of Billy, dear,"
　　The lady then replied,
As she then took the older boy
　　And drew him to her side.
Then Billy knelt down by the couch,
　　And Jacky's hand he took,
Saying, " You'll soon get well again !"
　　But Jacky did not look.
His eyes were fast becoming dim,
　　And stretching forth his hand,
" Mother," he cried, " I've—come—to—keep—
　　" Christmas—in—that—bright—land"—
And as he spoke, his head fell back
　　Upon the pillow there,
While on his face a smile still played.
　　His soul had gone to share
A better Christmas in the skies,
　　In mother's company ;
Where want and sorrow are unknown,
　　And all is bright and free.

And though some years have rolled along
　　Since Jacky passed away,
Yet still Bill strives to shun the wrong,
　　Hoping that he, some day,

Will meet dear Jack, and mother too,
  In mansions bright above—
Never to part, ever to join
  In singing Jesu's love.

DICK, THE CROSSING SWEEPER.

DICK was only a crossing sweeper,
  In one of the city streets ;
And he was so poor and friendless,
  That life to him had few sweets.

But one friend he had named Lily,
  Who sold flowers over the way ;
They were only plain and cheap ones,
  So she hadn't a grand display.

Yet she often wished she could buy some,
  Yes, just like those she had seen
In the hands of the ladies who pass'd her—
  Roses and ferns, rich and green.

Sometimes Dick would leave his crossing
  Awhile, and run to his friend ;
And she was always glad to see him,
  Just a few moments to spend.

For often they had cheered each other,
  In times of distress and grief,
And almost forgot all their troubles,
  In giving each other relief.

One day Dick ran over to Lily,
  And as they were talking she said,
" Dick, are you not fond of red roses ?"
  At this, he nodded his head,

Saying, " Yes, oh, yes ; I am very ;
  " They smell so sweetly, you know ;
" I wish I could buy yer some, Lily,
  "And I will do some day, somehow."

Then she laughed, and said it was nonsense ;
  But Dick said again and again
" I'll buy yer some bonniest red roses,
  "Just see if I don't."   And then

Away he ran back to his crossing,
  Resolving to save up his cash ;
And oft he repeated, " I'll buy 'em !
  "Then, oh, my ; she will cut a dash."

At the finish of that day's sweeping
  Dick felt much elated to know
That besides finding bed and supper
  He had threepence to spare, and so

He said to himself, " Now I'll buy cm ;"
  Then off to a shop right away
He ran, and there in the window
  He saw such a beautiful spray

Of red roses, and entering boldly
  He said to the lady inside,
" What's the price o' those 'eer red roses?"
  At which to him she replied,

And said with a smile, " Two and sixpence."
  Then Dick turned sadly away ;
For he'd set his heart on the purchase
  For Lily, " o' that 'eer bookay "—

   *   *   *   *   *   *   *

One morning the flower girl was absent,
  For, seized with a fever, she lay
On a wretched bed in a garret,
  And Dick missed her all that day.

So when his day's labor was ended,
  Though weary and footsore was he,
He resolved he would go and see her,
  For he knew he would welcome be.

But when he arrived at the garret,
  Poor Lily said eagerly,
" Dick ! Where are the beautiful roses,
  " The red ones, you promised to me?"

Then advancing a little nearer,
  He took her hot hand in his own—
Oh, how burning it was with the fever—
  And begged of her to lie down,

Saying, " I hav'nt the roses Lily,
  " I 'aint got the money yet ;
" But I promised, and I will buy 'em,
  " So there's a darling, don't fret."

Then poor Dick, both sad and bewildered,
  Stole away, with tears in his eyes ;
And wandering into the city,
  His heart well nigh burst with sighs,

He came at last to the flower shop,
  Where he'd been not long ago ;
And there again in the window
  Such beautiful roses he saw.

The young lady observed him looking,
  And stepping outside she said,
" Are you the boy who not long since
  "Called here ?" Dick nodded his head,

Saying, " Yes, I should like some roses,
  " For Lily, my friend, she's so ill ;
" But I know I 'aint enough money,"
  He said, as his eyes did fill

Again with tears. But, said the lady,
"How much have you got, my lad?"
"Two shillings," he said, rather slowly,
And he hung down his head, so sad.

"Come into the shop," she said, smiling,
"And from the best roses you see
"You may choose for yourself, for two shillings."
Then he entered the shop with glee.

 * * * * * * *

About ten minutes later our hero
Stood again in the garret's gloom ;
And, unwrapping the beautiful roses,
That with fragrance fill'd the room,

He stole to the bedside on tiptoe,
Thinking she must be asleep ;
And touching her gently, and softly,
Said, "Lily! Come, just take a peep

"At those lovely and charming red roses,
"I've brought them at last you see."
Then she opened her eyes, and saw them,
Crying, "Dick! Are they for me?"

And over her face, sad and weary,
A bright sunny smile there pass'd,
As she said, "Dear Dick, now I'm happy,
"I thought you would bring them at last."

Then she said, "Come, Dick, let me kiss you,"
And held up her thin wan face,
While the boy clasped his arms around her
In a fond and last embrace.

"Thank you, good night," then she murmured;
"I'm so tired and weary; but, dear,
"I feel Jesus, the Saviour, is near me,
"And I know I've nothing to fear.

"So good-night again, and God bless you"—
These were the last words she said;
And her eyes were then closed for ever,
And poor Dick knew she was dead!

She had gone to the home for poor children,
To a brighter and happier place;
Yes, gone with the scent of the roses
Lingering on her sweet face.

LITTLE NELL, OR THE ACROBAT'S REVENGE.

THE ground was covered thick with snow,
And fiercely keen the wind did blow,
As o'er a rough uneven road
The show vans creaked beneath their load—
'Twas a circus and a wild-beast show,
Combined in one, which often go
On tour, and on the village green
Or in the country town is seen—

At last they stop, and turn within
A waste enclosure, and begin
To pitch their tent; all hands are called
To take their part, and having hauled
The canvas roof, they spread it o'er
The open space, and scarce an hour
Has passed away before the tent
Is ready for the eve's event.

Five caravans there were in all,
Containing wild beasts great and small;
Others also, in which to stow
The costumes used within the show.
In one of these there lay a child,
Tossing with fever fierce and wild:
A little girl, but six years old,
With flaxen hair that shone like gold;

While close beside her on the bed
A woman sat with downcast head.
The tears were flowing from her eyes,
And from her breast heaved heavy sighs.
Sometimes, when conscious for awhile,
The child would raise her head and smile,
Which often eased her mother's care
And drove away her sad despair.

'Twas just three hours before the time
To start the show ; she heard the chime
Of village bell, tolling the hour—
She listened ; yes, 'twas striking four.
Just when the clock had ceased, a man
Appeared, whose face was pale and wan ;
And, as he came, with silent tread
He stole on tiptoe to the bed,
For he was careful, lest he might
Disturb the child—" How's Nell to-night ?"
He whispered to his wife ; for he
Was father to the girl.   And she
Replied—" I'm very much afraid
She's worse again "—then with her head
Bowed down she wept o'er little Nell ;
How great her sorrow none, could tell.

At last, Bob said, " I wonder who
" Will watch her while we're in the show ?"
" I cannot leave my darling's side,"
Replied his wife—" For woe betide
" Us if when we perform to-night
" Nell left her bed ; oh, that we might
" Just for this once permission get
" To stay with her.   The Boss might let
" Us off this night's performance, dear !
" Go ask him, Bob ! I know he's queer ;
" But tell him of the dangerous state
" Of Nell, and tell him that her fate,
" Her life, depends upon the care
" That we may now together share."

Then Bob to Mr. Hodgkins went
With heavy heart, and head low bent;
He knew, too well, 'twas vain to ask
The boss to let them off their task.
And so, when his appeal he made,
Hodgkins, in anger frowned, and said—
" I cannot help you, and if you
" Refuse to act to-night the two
" Of you must leave the show."   Bob then
In sadness turned away, and when
He told his wife the showman's words,
She wept, but said—" We can't afford
" To lose our place, and Nell so ill;
" Oh ! it is very hard ! Yet still   .
" We'll have to do our work somehow,
" Or he will turn us from the show."

So she and Bob performed that night
Upon the high trapeze.   The sight
Was one which drew large crowds ; both old
And young trudged through the biting cold
That winter's eve, for Bob's great skill
Was known.   The show began to fill,
And soon was packed.   At length the time
To start drew near.   The clock did chime
The hour of seven, when man and wife
Appeared upon the scene, and rife
With loud huzzas the tent did ring,
As up the ropes fast hurrying
They climbed on to the bars.   And when
The daring feats began the men
And boys rose from their seats, and loud
Were the shouts from the excited crowd.

But see ! within the tent a child
Appears, and very soon the wild
Huzzas are hushed—'Tis little Nell !
" Mother," she cries.   Oh ! who could tell
The feelings of that mother's heart—
" Mother, I'm afraid."   Then, a start !

A shriek! Bob's wife had failed to reach
The swinging bar, and, with a screech
Of wild despair, she headlong fell
Close by the side of little Nell,
And there upon the ground they lay
Quite still. At length the crowd give way
For Bob, who, having seen her fall,
Has left the trapeze bar. A pall
Of sad despair spreads o'er his face,
As down he kneels beside the place
Where his young wife is lying dead;
Then, sobbing loud, he bows his head
And cries, in anguish keen and wild,
" God, save my darling wife and child."

The people who had gathered round
Removed the child from off the ground —
For little Nell was also dead—
Her spirit from this world had fled —
And sought to keep the news so sad
From Bob, lest it should drive him mad,
Nor told him that poor little Nell
Had gone to live where angels dwell.
But he found out the worst ere long,
And soon he left th' excited throng —
Looking with rage and anger round,
He hastened off the Circus ground.

    *   *   *   *   *   *

When morning dawned two of the men
Walked round the caravans, and when
They came to where the showman slept,
And found the door ajar, they stept
Inside, and there upon the floor
Hodgkins lay dead, and covered o'er
With blood! While, from the footprints there,
They guess'd the cause of death. The bear
Had somehow got out of its den.
They turned towards Bruin's cage, and when

They gazed upon the fastenings saw
They had not been by Bruin's paw
Unloosed.   Who then had done the deed?
Some there were who guessed; none agreed;
" It was an accident " a few
Declared, but only one man knew.

" THE SHIPWRECK."
A STORY FOUNDED ON FACT.

'Twas on a dark and stormy night,
  Far, far away across the sea ;
No moon to shed her silvery light,
  The wind was blowing furiously.

Near to a wild and rocky coast,
  Huge waves beat high against the shore,
And in their madd'ning fury toss'd
  With noise loud as the thunder's roar.

Now and again the wind would cease,
  And for awhile was hushed and calm ;
Then suddenly it would increase,
  And e'en more wildly raged the storm.

But in those moments calm and still
  The people who lived near the sea
Heard cries for help, both loud and shrill,
  Which fill'd their hearts with misery.

And, though the darkness hid from view
  The ship from which was heard the cry,
The men upon the shore well knew
  A vessel was on rocks close by.

And so, throughout that dreadful night,
  They waited for the sun to rise ;
And when it cast its first faint light,
  A scene of terror met their eyes.

For on the rocks, not far from land,
    They saw a ship, almost a wreck ;
And, wildly waving with their hands,
    The passengers stood on the deck.

Their cries for aid rang through the air,
    Yet helpless was the crowd, though brave—
No lifeboat on the shore was there,
    No common boat their lives could save.

The people from the hills around
    Came crowding down upon the shore ;
Yet no assistance could be found,
    For none had seen such storm before.

At last the sound of hoofs was heard,
    And in the distance could be seen
A horseman, who at length appeared
    Riding with haste towards the scene.

The crowd immediately gave way,
    As from his horse the rider sprang,
And seized a rope without delay,
    While o'er the hills loud cheers now rang.

This man they knew had often braved
    The fiercest storms upon the sea,
And many a drowning one had saved—
    A hero bold and true was he.

The horse he rode was known as well—
    The wonder of the country round ;
Perfect in form, sound as a bell—
    None other like it could be found.

Just for a moment then he stood,
    To pat his favorite's archèd neck ;
Then glancing up in silent mood
    He turned his eyes towards the wreck.

What were his thoughts as he stood there?
  What scheme could he at once conceive ?
How could he through the breakers bear,
  And those in peril now relieve?

Then turning to his horse again,
  " Jenny," he said, " Shall we now try
To swim across the angry main?"—
  The horse then neighed in fond reply,

And looked into her master's eyes ;
  Then for a sign her head she bowed,
As on her back, amid the cries
  Of wonder from the excited crowd,

Without another word he sprang,
  And plunged into the raging deep—
" They will be lost," the cry now rang,
  And loudly did the people weep.

But no! They battle with the sea,
  And every moment brings them near
The doomed vessel, where they see
  The seamen clinging with despair.

At last they reach the vessel's side,
  And soon the rider springs on deck ;
Then to the horse the rope is tied,
  And next they're seen to leave the wreck.

While, clinging to the rope behind,
  A line of human beings is seen ;
Oh, can they hold 'gainst sea and wind?
  Or will they perish yet between

The ship and land? Grave doubts arise,
  Lest horse and man should fail to reach
The shore again—but mid surprise
  They soon are close upon the beach.

And now at length they gain the shore—
 The precious cargo safely lands ;
Oh, will they venture out for more ?
 For there now beckoning with their hands

Others upon the wreck they see
 Crying for help. Then to his steed,
He turns again—" Jenny "—says he—
 " We must unto their cries give heed."

So once again they face the storm,
 And battle with the wind and wave ;
They reach the ship, where white with foam
 The hero stands—resolved to save—

But, oh, it was a fearful thing,
 To see them plunging from the deck ;
Yet safe to land again they bring
 A precious cargo from the wreck.

And, as the people crowd around,
 Their loud huzzas ring through the air,
As yet again the hero turned
 Towards the wreck, for clinging there

A few remained,.whom he would try
 To rescue from a watery grave :
Who still were crying piteously
 And tossing helpless on the wave.

Once more he looked upon his horse,
 Her strength he knew was well nigh gone ;
Yet soon determined on his course—
 His love to man the victory won.

Then instantly he jumped astride
 His ever bold and gallant steed,
And plunged into the seething tide,
 Nor to the raging sea gave heed.

They swim again, though slowly on
   Towards the sinking ship; they reach
The vessel's side at last: " Well done "—
   Bursts from the crowd upon the beach.

Ere long each one the rope holds fast,
   And then into the sea they leap.
Oh ! Will they all be saved at last ?—
   Can man and horse their strength still keep ?

Ah ! What a fearful struggle—stay !
   They disappear ! Yet soon again
They rise ! Oh, will their strength give way
   And will this last attempt prove vain ?

Alas ! Alas ! A mightier wave
   Than all before above them rolls—
They sink ! And find a watery grave—
   No more are seen those precious souls.

And thus this noble-hearted man
   And faithful horse both perished there ;
While on the shore the tidings ran
   The people wept in deep despair.

And to this day, when storms beat high
   Upon that coast, the tale is told—
And many a strong man heaves a sigh,
   As he portrays that hero bold.

"BOB, THE FIREMAN, OR AN INCIDENT OF THE FIFTH OF NOVEMBER."

No ! Don't say that, sir, for it hurts me so—
I'd rather you gave me a cruel blow
Than speak like that of Bob ! 'Tis true his face
Is full of ugly scars.   Yet no disgrace
Are they to him ! Just listen, and I'll tell
You of the sad calamity, that fell

On Bob, the fireman, many years ago,
And how those dreadful scars came on his brow."

But ere this story I to you relate,
Perhaps it would be best, if I should state
The reason why those words above were said,
And what to this most touching story led.

'Twas on the "Fifth, Guy Fawkes' day," when I
Went for an evening's stroll, and passing by
The station of the Fire Brigade—I saw
A man in charge.   The air being cold and raw,
I stepped inside to have a smoke and chat,
And while away the time.   I scarce had sat
One minute, when a man appeared, whose face
Was dreadful to behold.   Hardly a trace
Of human form was left.   He nodded to
The fireman as he passed, then going through
A door, he disappeared.   I with a start
Exclaimed, " Oh ! What a monster."   Then a smart
Of conscience stung me, as I looked upon
The face of my companion.   In a tone
Of kind rebuke, he said, " Don't say that, sir ;
You don't know Bob, or you wouldn't, I'll aver—
For, though his face is ugly, yet his heart
Is good, and true, and brave ; for oft the part
That he has played in days gone by has shown
That he a hero was, and through the town
No man is honoured more.   No, he is not
A fireman now, though always on the spot
To lend a helping hand if needed.   He
And his wife—yes, he's married—and you see
They live in rooms above.   ' How's that ?' you say.
You'd like to hear the story ? Well, you may ;
It's just the night to tell it.   'Tis a tale
I've often told, and yet it ne'er grows stale."

The fireman then commenced this story to relate,
How, fifteen years that night, Bob met his fate.
" We sat down here, just as we two are now,

Smoking our pipes, when suddenly the blow
Of whistle sounded.   'Twas the well known call
To duty !   Two minutes later, and all
The men were ready for a start.   Then down
The horses madly galloped through the town.
Bob Anderson and I stood side by side,
And both were doubtless thinking of his bride ;
For, ere th' alarm was given, our quiet chat
Had been of Nelly Lee, and as we'd sat
Upon this very seat he'd told me all
About his coming marriage, while his tall
And well-built form had shook with laughter, when
At his request I'd promised there and then
To act as his best man.   And as we sped
Swiftly along the busy streets I said,
' I hope we shall not, on your wedding-day,
Travel so fast' ; and Bob turned round to say,
' Perhaps there will not be one, for may be
' That Nelly will not wed the likes o' me.'

Just at that moment, as the engine flew
Along the crowded streets, there came in view
A sight that almost staggered us.   I guess
There was no more time for talk, for in less
Than half a minute, sir, we heard the cries
Of them poor wretches for help, while our eyes
Took in their peril at a glance ; for there,
Clinging to the windows, in wild despair,
Both men and women stood.   I should have told
You, sir, it was a lodging-house, where old
And young were staying on that awful night ;
Nor shall I e'er forget the dreadful sight.

The fire, which started in the rooms below,
Had not yet reached the upper floor, and now
The engine stopp'd : and, sir, I never knew
Our chaps get quicker into business.   Few
Fire brigades could equal us, for our men
Were strong and brave, and so I need not then

Describe how hard we worked to rescue those
Poor precious lives. At last the cry arose
That all were saved, but soon we heard a shrill
And piercing shriek for help, and on the sill
Of window in the topmost room we saw
A woman with a child. A thrill of awe
Then ran through every heart.

And now ere long
The tongues of flame had reached her, and among
The cries below, her voice was heard, " Oh! save
My child!" 'Twas then Bob Anderson the brave
Appeared, and up the longest ladder he
Sprang quickly, while the crowd tremendously
Then cheered him. But ere he gained her side,
With a wild cry, which echoed far and wide,
She shrieked again, " Oh! Save my child," and then
She threw it down below; but two strong men
Received it in their arms, both safe and sound,
Or 't would have fallen dead upon the ground.
The woman swooned, and back she fell, ere Bob
Could reach the window-sill. A bitter throb
Of grief and woe then shook the crowds below,
For Bob had also disappeared. And now
The smoke and flames each moment thicker grew,
And both, alas! were hidden from our view—
Yet not for long, for suddenly I saw
A blackened form appear again, and lo!
Within his arms Bob Anderson now bore
The woman he had gone to save. While o'er
The gaping crowd deep silence reigned, until
With scarce a moment's pause I with a will
Undaunted up the ladder quickly climbed,
And first I seized the woman's form, begrimed
With smoke, and scorched with fire; then passed
      her down
To those below—she was not dead, and soon
Both Bob and I were safely on the ground;
But he, poor fellow, sad to tell, was found
So sadly burned he had to be conveyed

Unto the hospital, where it was said
He never would be cured. *   *   *   *   *

A week had passed,
And I had been unconscious, but at last
I learned Bob's fate: He had the shock survived,
And almost by a miracle he lived—
Yet not the Bob I saw that eve ascend
The fire-escape ; for when I found my friend
In hospital I there beheld a being
Whose face I hardly recognized. And seeing
Him I wept aloud with grief— *   *   *   *   *

Months had fled,
And then one day a message came, which said
That Anderson was ready then to leave
The hospital. So off I went to receive
And welcome back my friend. I scarce can tell
The deep emotions of my heart, for well
I knew that Nelly Lee, his love and pride,
Would be ashamed to see him at her side.
And so it proved, for Nell had scarcely seen
His sad disfigured face, when she had been
To visit him, as he unconscious lay,
Nor thought that with the change would pass away
Her love for him, yet so it was ; and when
He went to see her, why she there and then
Refused to look at him. So all was up
Between them, and poor Bob his bitter cup
Drank to the dregs, bidding to life's fond dream
Of happiness farewell—

This was to him
More cruel far than anything beside,
And oft he wished he in the fire had died—

But time passed on, and Bob grew strong again,
Yet I could see his heart was filled with pain ;
And, though a pension granted by the town
Provided for his wants, yet he had grown

More melancholy still; for oft he heard
The lads cry out, ' Guy Fawkes, Guy Fawkes '—which
    stirred
His heart with grief.

                But I must hurry on
And finish up my tale. It chanced upon
Another night, just four years after that
On which Bob met his fate. And as I sat
And thought of days gone by, who should appear
But Bob! I should have told you, sir, that here
He often came to lend a helping hand,
Though not a regular member of the band.
Well, scarce five minutes pass'd, before we heard
Th' alarum ring, and up we jumped and stirred
Ourselves. The fire was in a well-known square—
So Bob at once resolved to go, for there
Lived Nelly Lee. And, as we dashed away
Along the crowded streets, I heard him say,
' I wonder if it's Nellie's home?' His face,
Though marred, was bright and beaming, not a trace
Of fear was there, and very soon we came
In sight of Portland Square. To Bob the name
Had precious been, in days gone by ; and now
As we arrived, and saw the fierce flames glow,
He cried, ' 'Tis Nelly's father's shop!' ' Come men,'
He yelled; ' Come, hurry up! look sharp!' and then
He shouted out, " These folks are friends of mine."
' Yes, pretty friends,' we thought. But at the sign
From Bob, each man worked with a will. The fire
Was gaining ground, and soon the flames leaped higher,
And then 'twas seen that nothing now could save
The house and shop from ruin. Yet bold and brave
The firemen worked, assisted by the crowd,
To save whate'er they could.

                Just then a loud
And piercing cry was heard, " O save my child."
'Twas the voice of Mr. Lee, whose face was wild
With deep despair, for Nell had disappeared

Within the burning shop, and it was feared
She would be lost.

      It seems that she had gone
To fetch her father's cash-box, and upon
Reaching the upper room, where it was kept,
Had turned to bring it down.   The fire had crept
Up through the staircase, and the flames arose
And beat her back.   'Twas then, so I suppose,
She thought of Bob, for she had seen
The bold and fearless man, as he had been
Urging the men to rescue all they could,
And save her father's property.   She stood
For a moment, then to the window went,
And soon above the din the air was rent
With a loud voice: "Oh! save me, Bob!" cried she.
Bob heard her voice, and like a hero he
Sprang up the fire-escape, and in his arm
He bore her gently down, quite free from harm.

No, she wasn't hurt, and since I've heard her say
That all her former love returned that day
As she felt Bob's arm around her ; and when
The fire was out I found them once again
As thick as two young turtle doves.

      And now
I think, sir, you will guess the ending—How
A short time after, they were wed.   And I,
O yes, was Bob's best man.   And, sir, that's why
I always speak a word for Bob, my friend."

—Just as he brought his story to an end,
A chubby little chap, some six years old,
Came trotting in—his hair, which shone like gold,
Hung round his neck in curls.   "And who is this?"
I asked.   "Why Bob's youngest child."   Then a kiss.
"Hark ye! he calls me uncle ; I forgot
To tell you I wed his sister, Charlotte—

No, sir; don't apologise," he smiling said,
" I know you meant no harm."   And then he led,
Me up the stairs, saying, " I'll introduce
" You to my friends above."   And there, all spruce
And neat, they sat around the fireside grate,
And glad were they to see me.

                         Need I state,
As I now end my story sad, but true,
That when I pass that way, as I oft do,
I always step inside, my friends to see,
And with a smile they gladly welcome me.

STORM AT SEA.

In an old fishing village, lying near the sea,
On the Eastern Coast of Yorkshire, I chanced to be
Once staying with a friend. I had gone there to rest,
Also for change of air ; and hailing from the West,
From a large and crowded city, I quickly found   [round
My health was much improved, and as the weeks went
I and my friend together often took a walk,
To smoke an evening pipe, and have a quiet talk.

I can remember well, though years have roll'd away,
A fearful storm one night, as if 'twere yesterday—
Oh, such a storm ! I fancy I can see it now,
And seem as if I felt the wild winds fiercely blow.

'Twas in the Autumn, and the day had been quite calm,
Just such a day as oftentimes precedes a storm—
The sun was sinking, and the Western sky shone red
As if 'twere bathed in liquid fire. The mountain's head
Was crowned with crimson glow. The sea appeared at
        rest.
Th' aquatic birds swam gently o'er its placid breast.
The fishermen had drawn their boats high on the beach,
And, as they homeward walked and heard the sea-gulls
        screech,

They gravely shook their heads in ominous dismay,
Saying, "There'll be a storm, before the break of day."

Ere long a change was seen—the sky became o'ercast
With heavy sable clouds, the moaning wind at last
Began to blow a gale.   The lightning's flash we saw !
We heard the distant thunder peal; and struck with awe,
We hastened to the village, from which my friend and I—
Not thinking of the gathering storm, or darkening sky—
Had wandered far away ; but ere it came in view
The rain in torrents poured, the wind much fiercer blew.
And as we hastened on, drawing towards the sea,
We saw the foaming billows dashing furiously
Upon the rocks below ; then trembling at the sight,
We prayed—"God help the men, who on the sea to-night
Are battling with the waves."   And as we gazed upon
The seething foam, we heard, distinct and clear, a gun,
Which, very well we knew, came from some vessel doomed.
For, as the lightning flashed ! and bellowing thunder
          boomed !
We in the distance saw a helpless ship being driven
Upon the surging sea, with sails in tatters riven.
Then coming towards the beach, over the village green,
The fishermen now ran, for they had also seen
The vessel in distress.   And with them they did bring
Their stoutest ropes and life-buoys, while we, hurrying
Through the blinding storm to meet them, could plainly
          see
The ship was drifting to the rocks, then piteously,
Loud cries for help were heard, rising above the sound
Of wind and waves. At once the men, with ropes around
Their waists, dashed through the surf towards the
          helpless craft,
Where, clinging to the vessel's masts, both fore and aft,
Were seen the shipwrecked crew.   And then again we
          prayed
"God save these helpless men "—E'en as these words
          were said
The doomèd vessel reeled ! and on the rocks was cast,
A hopeless wreck ! but on the surging waves the mast

And rigging tossed, while clinging to them could be seen
Two brave and stalwart men, and holding up between
Them in their brawny arms they bore a little child—
It was the captain's child—" Oh save us!" loud and wild
The cry rang out from these brave men.—A rope was
    thrown,
They seized it and were saved. But all the rest went down,
And with the ship were lost. So doth my story end ;
Yet often, when I pay a visit to my friend,
In sadness we refer to that most awful sight,
Nor shall we e'er forget the storm that Autumn night.

ADVICE TO BOYS.
"SPEAK A KIND WORD WHEN YOU CAN."

JUST speak a kind word when you can, boys,
    For there's many a heart full of sadness
That you might relieve with a word, boys,
    And sorrow would change into gladness.

" Kind words never die," it is said, boys,
    Though they may, for awhile, not be heeded;
Yet some day they'll bring their reward, boys,
    And prove just the words that were needed.

How many there are who require, boys,
    A few words which are loving and cheering,
To help them in shunning the wrong, boys,
    And save them from rocks they are nearing.

For many are tempted to sin, boys,
    Who for help are constantly calling ;
And if you keep on the look-out, boys,
    Perchance you'll prevent them from falling.

And if you but once should succeed, boys,
    In saving a soul that is erring,
You never again would be found, boys,
    Kind words to the needy deferring.

"ADVICE TO GIRLS."

In walking the pathway through life, girls,
    You must be sure and keep a straight line ;
Nor swerve to the right or the left, girls,
    But the wiles of the tempter decline.

For often there lurks in the way, girls,
    Many dangers you cannot behold ;
And if you step out of the path, girls,
    It will lead you to sorrows untold.

Then be careful as each step you take, girls,
    And let virtue your motto remain ;
That your life in the future may be, girls,
    Kept free from impurity's stain.

And if this advice you will keep, girls,
    You shall reap a rich harvest of joy ;
And receive an eternal reward, girls,
    Where no tempter can ever destroy.

MY MOTHER.

Whose voice, when in my childhood's years,
In sweetest tones allayed my fears ;
Whose soft hand wiped away my tears ?
                        My Mother's.

Who nursed me when, with parchèd tongue,
And fever'd brow, nigh death I hung ;
And softest lullabies then sung ?
                        My Mother.

Who heard me lisp my feeble prayers,
And soothed my sorrows, and my cares ;
Who guarded me 'mid youthful snares ?
                        My Mother.

Who shielded me amid the strife,
Which in my boyhood's days was rife ;
Who pointed out the path of life ?

My Mother.

Who, when in sad distress and grief,
Brought to my troubled heart relief,
And made the hours seem bright and brief ?

My Mother.

But well do I remember, how
At length she lay with fevered brow ;
'Twas then I cried, in pain and woe,

My Mother !

And, oh ! what bitter tears I shed,
When kneeling by the silent bed,
On which was lying cold and dead,

My Mother.

*　　　*　　　*　　　*　　　*　　　*

And now, though years have passed away,
And she lies mouldering with the clay,
I gaze upon her grave, and say,

My Mother !

ADVICE TO THE YOUNG.

In climbing the ladder of fame,
　If you would successful prove,
And win for yourselves a great name,
　Be careful as each step you move.

For many there are who begin,
　And climb very well for a time ;
But soon they are tempted by sin
　And fail ere life's at its prime.

In climbing the ladder of life,
   Make the first rung your desire ;
And you will gain strength in the strife,
   As you mount up those that are higher.

For that's the way all men have done,
   Who've climbed to the top with success,
Who the nation's best plaudits have won,
   And God delighted to bless.

Let Excelsior your motto remain,
   And fearless your efforts to rise ;
Then you shall successfully gain
   The fame and the honour you prize.

And, if through life's pathway you keep
   The advice to you we now give,
For the fruit of your toil you shall reap
   The hero's reward, while you live.

SCRIPTURE NARRATIVES

IN RHYME.

THE PHARISEE AND THE PUBLICAN.

Wrapt in the splendour of an Eastern sky,
The pinnacled towers of the proud city lie ;
In majestic repose, unconscious of danger,
She slumbers nor heedeth the voice of the Stranger,
         Who tells of her doom.

    ✻   ✻   *   ✻   ✻   *

The ninth hour of the day is fast drawing near,
And the streets, which where silent, now busy appear ;
To the Temple far-famed, eager feet are approaching
To offer their sacrifice—No business encroaching—
         On that sacred hour.

Men of all ranks and grades obey the sacred call,
And through the Temple gates are passing all—
But see ! Here cometh one who in rank is surely higher
Than all who yet have passed—Is he a saintly sire,
         That thus he comes ?

With slow majestic tread he draweth nigh,
Ascends the polished steps, and stands on high—
Within the sacred precincts of Jehovah's Temple ;
Truly a man of noble presence, an example
         To all around.

Who is this worshipper? Doubtless some Jewish Prince—
Or a man of high authority—And hence
How lordly his mien, his aspect how commanding—
How conscious of his dignity—thus demanding
         Our attention.

Also a man of wealth, for he is richly dress'd—
A robe of finest texture is hung across his breast;
And among the folds of his silken turban gleaming
Are jewels both bright and rare, sparkling and beaming
         'Neath the sun's bright rays.

Nay, more, he is a man of sanctity, for see
How deep and broad the hem of his garments be,
While on the marble floor his embroidered robe is flowing
And on his forehead bound are texts of Scripture—showing
         His zeal for the truth.

He is a Pharisee, a man of righteousness,
Also a man of impregnable holiness!
Behold! an example of human perfection—
Of unblemished purity—a reflection
         Of pure godliness.

       *   *   *   *   *   *

And now the white-robed priests their sacred call attend,
While, densely thick, the clouds of incense rich ascend—
On the assembled throng deep silence reigns supremely,
As the Pharisee composed, with outward form so seemly,
         Prepares to pray.

But stay! We hear the sound of footsteps drawing near,
Which break upon the solemn stillness resting there—
Whoever can it be, that dares so late to enter
Into the holy temple, and thus to venture
         Within the sacred shrine?

See, through the archèd doorway, in dark-hued garments
Enters a man with face so sorrowful and sad ;   [clad,
Slowly he moves along, with shame and sorrow bending—
His eyes are downward cast—No pomp his steps
          He is a Publican.   [attending—

Into the darkest corner, slowly and sadly steals
This poor despised Publican—What misery he feels—
No place is there for him, where the sun is brightly
          streaming
So richly on the pavement stones, and beaming
          So brilliantly.

The spot on which the Pharisee stands with form erect
Is not the place for him, whom no one doth respect—
If nothing else would keep him from showing his emotion,
The look of that bold worshipper would hinder his devotion,
          And crush his burdened soul.

So he standeth afar off, nor dares to glance to heaven—
With downcast head, and his heart with anguish riven,
He smites upon his breast—And yet in hope relying
On Him who reads the heart, with earnest fervour crying,
          " Be merciful to me."

But hark !   The Pharisee has now begun to pray ;
And, as with folded arms he stands, we hear him say—
" God, I thank Thee, I'm not as other men, not even
" As this Publican "—But will the God of heaven
          Listen to such mockery ?

No! No! His pompous words fall back again to earth,—
A vast emptiness—to which his pride gave birth—
His false devotions end, and, with a haughtier bearing
Than before, he leaves the holy Temple, daring
          To think himself secure.

Oh! Blind Pharisee! And canst thou thus presume
Upon Jehovah's mercy? Then listen to thy doom—
"He that exalteth himself, and seeks to merit heaven,
"Shall be abased" by God, and from his presence driven
          To everlasting woe!

The Publican now leaves the Temple's sacred shrine—
How radiant beams his face, so full of joy divine—
And as with cheerful step he seeks his humble dwelling
He hears an inward voice, in tones of peace revealing—
          "Thou art justified."

These words our Saviour spake to those who put their trust
In outward rites and forms, yet were to men unjust :
"This man went down in peace"—for thus it is recorded—
"He that humbleth himself shall be by God rewarded
          "With everlasting life."

CHRIST STILLING THE TEMPEST.

'Twas night, and on the Sea of Galilee
     A ship was tossing on the billowy wave ;
The crew were fearful, lest they soon might be
     Cast on the deep, and find a watery grave.

A little while before, the sea was calm,
     As in the boat they sprang, and left the shore ;
But suddenly upon them came the storm,
     Nor had they seen such storm-tossed waves before.

They battled with the wind and waves until
     Their strength had well nigh gone, but all in vain—
The storm still raged—the boat began to fill,
     Yet on they toiled upon the angry main.

At last they cried for help—"Oh! Master! Save
     Us, or we perish in the yawning deep"—
For, there was One, whose power could still the wave—
     But, worn and weary, He lay fast asleep.

Yet, at this cry, He rose and with His word
    He hushed the winds, and bade the billows cease—
And straightway there was calm, for Christ the Lord
    The stormy sea controlled, and there was peace.

And often we, upon the sea of life
    Are tossed about by angry winds that blow,
Yet we forget, amid the toil and strife,
    That there is *One* to whom we then can go ;

And, if we cry for help, we soon shall find
    The Master at our side, whose voice can still
The raging sea control, and calm the wind,
    For they do yet obey the Saviour's will.

THE BIRTH OF CHRIST.

'Twas midnight, and over Bethlehem's plains there reigned
Deep silence, nor could a sound be heard, save perhaps
The distant night bird's screech, or dismal howl of wolf
In search of prey, which, to appease their hunger leave
Their darkest haunts, and fly, or prowl into the night—
That they perchance may find a poor stray lamb, or sheep,
Which, having wandered far beyond the shepherd's care,
Has lost itself amid the tangled briers and thorns.

Upon these plains, in deepest solitude, there watched
The shepherds by their flocks, when suddenly a blaze
Of light upon them came, and, falling to the ground,
Trembling with fear they lay, nor had they strength to rise,
Till listening they heard a voice distinct and clear,
Which bade them " Fear not "—While looking up they
    saw
The plains were lit with splendour, that exceeded far
The noonday's sun in brightness, for around them shone
" *The Glory of the Lord* "—And 'mid the dazzling rays
An Angel stood, who thus proclaimed the Saviour's birth.

" Behold I bring glad tidings of great joy to all,
"For unto you is born this day of *David's line*
" *A Saviour*, which is *Christ the Lord*, and for a sign,
"In Bethlehem's manger laid, you there shall find the *babe*
" In swaddling clothing wrapp'd."   Then suddenly there
      joined
A multitude of heavenly hosts, who sang God's praise,
And made the distant hills re-echo with their song.

The shepherds then arose from off the ground, entranc'd
With joy ! for all their fears had fled, and hastening
Away they went to see the *Babe* in Bethlehem.
Nor did they stop, till they beheld with wondering eyes
The infant Christ—Whom having seen, returned at once
The joyful tidings to make known to all around.

And although eighteen hundred years and more have
      pass'd
Since Christ our Saviour's birth by angels was proclaim'd
On Bethlehem's plains, yet still we hail with joyful song
Each Christmas day, and join in sweetest strains, to make
The Anthem swell again, as we the happy morn
Now greet which brings the tidings of the Saviour's birth—
While often do our hearts with love and joy o'erflow
To Him who came on earth salvation to bestow.

THE PARABLE OF THE SOWER.

BEHOLD !   A sower went forth to sow,
And, as he scattered the seed amain :
     Some fell by the wayside,
     But did not long abide ;
For the fowls picked up the fallen grain.

Some fell on stony ground, and these soon
Sprang up.   But when the sun's cheering rays
     Should have fed and cherished,
     They were scorched and perished ;
For they had no roots and withered away.

And some were sown among the thorns,
Which soon sprang up and choked the seed.
    So no fruit did these bear,
    For they could not grow there,
'Mid the tangling briers, and the clinging weeds.

But others fell on ground that was good,
And they brought forth fruit, not weeds or tares :
    Some brought forth sixty-fold,
    Others an hundred-fold,
For so God's word unto us declares.

" Who hath ears to hear, then let him hear,"
Our Saviour to the disciples said ;
    For they could not perceive,
    Neither could they believe,
Till in their minds His wisdom He shed.

And then He explained the parable thus—
" When any man heareth these words of mine,
    " And he knoweth them not,
    " Then the seed he hath got
" The wicked one taketh by foul design."

This is the man whom our Lord compares
To the wayside hearer, whose heart is hard ;
    For he doth not believe,
    Neither doth he receive
The words that are preached, nor reap the reward.

The next one is he who heareth the word,
And anon receives it without delay :
    This is the stony ground,
    Where not much earth is found,
And soon it withers, and parcheth away.

Then he that receiveth seed among thorns
Is he whom the world with riches deceives ;
    And his holy desires
    'Mid the tangling briers
Are choked, and bring forth nothing but leaves.

But he that receiveth into good ground
Is he that heareth and doth understand
    The life-giving word,
    And fruit to the Lord
Even an hundred-fold spreads o'er the land.

LET NOT YOUR HEARTS BE TROUBLED.

" LET not your hearts be troubled,"
    Were the words the Saviour said—
As He spake to His disciples,
    Whose hopes were withered and dead.

They were gathered there in sadness,
    In the hush of eventide ;
And their hearts were full of sorrow,
    Though Jesus was at their side.

Do you ask, " What made them fearful ?"
    Or enquire, " Why so sad were they ?"
It was because their Lord and Master
    Had said He was going away.

But Jesus bade them be cheerful—
    And a promise to them He did give—
" I go to prepare a place for you,
    "And with me ye then shall live."

" If ye love me, keep my sayings,
    " And I to my Father will pray ;
" That He may send the Comforter,
    " Who shall ever with you stay."

Then be not afraid to tarry
    Awhile in this world below,
For He, your Teacher, will guide you,
    And heal all your grief and woe.

"CHRIST RAISING THE WIDOW'S SON."

OUT, through the city gates, a funeral train
Is passing on and slowly moves along,
While, following close behind, a widowed mother
Treads with feeble step and tottering limbs ;
And as she walks, with head bowed down, she weeps
Such bitter tears, which, falling to the ground,
Call forth the deepest sympathy of those
Who with her follow on towards the tomb.

This weeping woman's heart is torn with grief,
For on that funeral bier they carry forth
Her son, her only son, who long had been
The joy and comfort of her life, and who
Had often cheered her in her great distress :—
For many years on him she had relied,
And on him built her future hope and joy ;
But now her hope had fled, her joy was gone—
For he, her darling son, lay withered, dead !
Seized by the mortal foe in manhood's prime,
A corpse he lies, and in the silent grave
Must soon be placed to moulder in the dust.

But hark !   A voice is heard, a voice so full
Of sympathy and love, that says, " Weep not."
And going to the bier on which the young man lay,
The Saviour touched it (for He it was who
Bade the widow's tears be dry).   And the men
Who bore the bier stood still, and wondered at
The stranger's words.   Then, with that voice which
        wakes
The sleeping dead, He cried ! " Young man ; I say
"To thee, ' Arise !' "   And straightway he, who had
Been dead, rose up with life and power renewed
To cheer again his widowed mother's breast
And help life's burden to remove, and thus
Bring joy and happiness where deep despair
Had dwelt, and banish sorrow, fear and care.

And so may we amid life's sorrows find
In Him our Comforter—for still He lives—
Though now we cannot see His loving face
Or hear His gentle voice (as in the flesh),
We yet by faith must trust His power to save
Us in the darkest hour of life, e'en when
The cold and icy hand of death removes
Our loved ones from our midst, and o'er the grave
We bend, and listen to the sad, sad words
Which sound upon our ears, " Dust unto dust."
For has He not declared in words of truth,
" I am the Resurrection and the Life."
And he who thus believes shall live again
In that eternal world of peace and joy.

CHRIST FEEDING THE MULTITUDES.

ALL through the long and dreary day
    The busy crowds the Saviour press'd;
They heeded not the sun's hot ray—
    But followed on—nor thought of rest.

They listened to His loving voice,
    His miracles Divine they saw—
They heard Him bid sad hearts rejoice !
    And banish all their grief and woe.

But now, the shades of eventide
    Are gathering o'er them, thick and fast:
Yet still they linger at his side,
    Although the day is nearly past.

Th' disciples then to Jesus went,
    And bade Him send the crowds away;
" The day," they said, " is now far spent,
    "Nor can they longer with us stay."

But " Christ, the Lord," compassion had,
    And heeded not the loud complaint
Of His disciples.   So he said,
    " Give them to eat, lest they should faint."

Then the disciples stood aghast!
  Nor understood their Lord's reply.
And so, with great surprise, they asked—
  " How can we, Lord, their needs supply ?"

" Two hundred pennyworth of bread,
  " Would not for them sufficient be."
For they forgot, how He had fed
  The multitudes in Galilee.

But when the people gathered round—
  He bade them place the hungry crowd
In fifties down upon the ground,
  And then His sacred head He bowed.

Then blessing, brake the five small loaves
  And two small fishes — all they had—
Thus Jesus fed the multitudes,
  And made their hearts feel light and glad.

" About five thousand " did partake
  Of bread and fish—till all were filled,
While, as the food our Saviour brake,
  It multiplied just as He willed.

" And when the fragments which remained
  " Were gathered up," behold, 'twas found
The bread and fish so much had gained—
  That great surprise was felt around.

Thus often did the Saviour show—
  In times of need—His wondrous power,
And willingly did He bestow
  His aid in many a trying hour.

And, though 'tis eighteen hundred years
  Since Christ His miracles displayed,
He still will banish all our fears
  If we but ask Him for His aid.

POEMS ON THE SEASONS.

—

SPRING.

—

SPRING'S AWAKING.

The winter's snow again has disappeared—
The sun pours forth it's warm and cheering rays—
While Nature greets its resurrecting power,
And with new life the hedgerows and the trees
Are clothed once more in Spring's habiliments.
The tiny flowers peep from their grassy beds,
And with their lovely tints of varied hue
The vales are deck'd.   And as we walk along
The meadow's path, we tread with careful step,
Lest carelessly we crush beneath our feet
The primrose or the violet, which fill
The morning air with perfume.

                              Suddenly
The sweet and joyous harbingers of spring
With songs enchanting greet our ears : the thrush
In yonder tree is warbling forth his notes,
Both shrill and clear, in joyful melody—
The skylark mounts on lofty wings, and soars
Into the air, trilling its merry tune,
And adds its cheerful tribute to the sun,
Which, rising in the Eastern sky, illumines
The earth with splendour, shedding its bright rays
O'er mountain, hill, and dale.

And as we gaze
Upon the handiwork of God, our hearts
Are filled with rapture, and with heaven-born joy;
While chords of harmony within our souls
Are touched as by skill'd fingers on the harp—
And mingling with the rippling rivulet,
Which sparkling flows beside the grassy bank,
Or blending with the voice of singing bird,
We join in songs of praise to Him whose power
And goodness fill the earth.

But language fails,
And poets in their happiest muse can ne'er
Portray the feelings of a sincere soul,
Who thus doth meditate upon His works;
Nor can the pen of mortal man describe—
Howe'er inspired—the joy and love which flow
In full and copious streams to God, who is
The Author and the Giver of all good.

"THE THRUSH": A MARCH SONG.

Welcome, sweet bird, thou harbinger of spring;
Thy tuneful notes sweet joy and gladness bring;
Soon as the dawn appears in Eastern sky,
We hear thy voice in cheerful melody.

Again at eve, as sinks the sun to rest
Behind the western hills, in crimson vest;
And as the man of toil, with weary tread,
Returns unto his cot with upturned head

He greets thy joyous song; for soon he knows
That winter's stormy winds and chilling snows
Shall disappear, while spring returns again,
Bringing its sunshine and its gentle rain,

Sing on, thou king of songsters, for thy mate
Is listening to thy warbling, sat in state
On topmost branch of yonder lofty tree;
And, as she hears thy evening's lullaby,

She for thy coming waits—just as the bride
Awaits the coming home, at eventide,
Of him, whose cheerful song and welcome voice
Bring peace, and make her loving heart rejoice.

LINES ON SPRING.

The winter's storms again have pass'd away, and Spring
Once more asserts her power, and with her mantle green
She decks each mountain, hill and dale. New life is seen
Displayed where'er the eye may turn, while that which
          seemed
Decayed and dead, bursts forth again with life renewed.
And we behold the trees, which but as yesterday
Were bare, and showed their naked twigs, to-day are
          clothed
In garb of varied hue, and soon will blossom forth
In promise of the fruitful harvest that shall come.

The meadows everywhere are decked with flowers so
          gay—
The daisy peeps out of its bed, and opens wide
Its tiny bloom to greet the morning sun. The primrose
And the violets, too, their carpets rich have spread,
Which fill the air with sweet perfume. While over all
The gentle zephyr wafts its cool refreshing breeze,
Imparting life and health to everything around.

The birds on bush and tree trill out their merry song,
And sweetest music greets our ears, as warbling forth
In lofty tuneful notes, each one unto its mate,
Their voices ring again, while echoes answer back
In sweet refrain, and thus doth joy and gladness spring
Into our hearts, then bursting forth in thankfulness

And praise to Him whose hand directs the Seasons in
Their course, and who decrees not one of them shall fail
While time on earth endures, our heartfelt songs now
    blend
In tuneful harmony to God who reigns above.

WELCOME SPRING.

Hail ! gentle, sweet and lovely Spring,
    We welcome thee again ;
Thou mak'st the song of gladness ring,
    O'er mountain, hill and plain.

With tints of rich and varied hue,
    Thou deck'st the landscape o'er ;
And, with thy touch, appears in view
    Each tiny bud and flower.

The meadow's carpet green is spread,
    On which the lambkins run,
And gambol, frisk, and jump ahead,
    Or bask beneath the sun.

The primrose and the violets shed
    Their perfume through the air ;
The daisies peep out of their bed,
    Thy cheering rays to share.

The thrush his merry song now sings
    In notes both clear and sweet ;
The skylark mounts on lofty wings,
    The morning's dawn to greet.

The cuckoo now, from milder climes,
    Returns across the sea,
And warbles forth in welcome chimes
    Its plaintive melody.

And in the hush of eventide
  The nightingale doth trill
Its evening songs, which far and wide
  The vales with music fill.

All nature thus proclaims again,
  In one united song,
Thy advent, while in soft refrain
  Its echoes we prolong.

SPRINGTIDE THOUGHTS AT SUNRISE.

THE morning dawns, and o'er the mountain top
The sun is gently rising, and will soon,
In his majestic splendour, shed his light
O'er hill and dale, on woodland and on plain—
Cov'ring with golden rays each forest tree,
And decking every tiny shrub and flower
With beauteous beams, which, mingling with the dew,
Will sparkle forth like jewels bright and rare.

The birds lift up their heads from 'neath their wings,
And rise to greet with joy the new-born day;
Then mounting on swift pinions through the air
Make hill and dale re-echo with their songs.

The little lambs begin to frisk and jump
In merry gambols o'er the meadows green,
And, with their unhorn'd heads, they butt and toss
Each other in their wantonness and play.

The labourer wakes, and, rising from his bed,
He bids dull sleep begone, then forth he goes
With cheerful step his daily bread to win.
And, as with sunny smile or merry song
He wends his way into the fields beyond—
Made mellow by the winter's frost and snow—
He takes the seed and spreads it o'er the land;
Nor does he doubt that, when the summer's sun

Hath shed abroad its warm and cheering rays,
A rich and plenteous harvest it will yield.
For God hath promised in His sacred word—
" That they who sow shall reap "—And here we learn
A lesson, which should regulate our life,
For all are sowing, either wheat or tares,
And all will, too, a harvest reap.   Oh, may
The seed we sow, whether mid smiles or tears,
Be sown in faith and hope : so shall we gain,
In God's own time, the fruit of all our toil,
And when the last great reaping time appears
And angels shall descend to gather in—
At God's command—the ripe and golden grain,
We shall be found among the wheat, not tares,
And hear the welcome shout of " Harvest Home."

SUMMER.

SUMMER THOUGHTS.

THE summer's sun shines brightly, and the sky
Is blue and clear, nor flits a cloud across
Its wide expanse.   The soft air wafts its smile
O'er hill and dale, and sweetest perfume spreads
Around our path, as we through meadows tread
With light and joyous step, e'en careful, lest
Our feet should trample on the smallest flower
That blooms, which lifts its tiny head to catch
The sunbeams as they fall.   And as we gaze
Upon the lovely scene, our hearts are filled
With joy, and songs of praise our lips employ.

The birds, in bush and tree, are warbling forth
In sweetest strains their morning songs to Him
Who is the giver of all good, Whose will
Commands the seasons as they come and go

Each one in its appointed course, for He
Hath said while time endures it shall be so ;
Not one of them shall fail—seed time, harvest,
Spring, Summer, Autumn, Winter, follow
In their successive rounds :—sunshine after rain ;
Plenty follows want ; rest treads on the heels
Of toil ; and all in turn give evidence
Of the Almighty power of Him, whose wisdom
Truth and goodness eternally display
That " God is love "—while we with joyful song
His praise prolong in one united strain.

THE JOY OF HARVEST.

HARVEST time, glad harvest time, again is here ;
The corn is ripe, and bends its full and laden ear;
Where'er the eye can reach, the rich and golden grain
Is ready for the reaper's sythe, and once again
The joyous shout, the shout of " Harvest Home," is heard,
And, listening to the sound, our hearts with joy are stirred.

The trees are filled again with ripening fruits, and bend
Beneath their weight, while lovely flowers their fragrance
            blend
And fill the air with perfume rich and rare, while all
Around, on hill, through dale, the voice of nature calls
For gratitude and love to Him who rules for good,
And who provides His creatures year by year with food.

Then raise again the shout of " Harvest home," and make
The hills and valleys ring, as ye your offerings take
From out your bounteous stores ; and as ye thus present
Your tithes to Him, and in pure adoration bent,
Let gladness fill your hearts, and words of praise employ
Your noblest powers in songs of everlasting joy.

AUTUMN.

AN AUTUMNAL REVERIE.

THE Autumn leaves were falling fast,
  The wind blew cold and chill,
As through the woodland glade I passed
  Beside the rippling rill.

A few short weeks before, the dell
  With music soft and sweet
Re-echoed, and its magic spell
  Had stayed my wandering feet.

But now the songs of birds were hushed,
  And nothing could be heard
Save the rustling of the falling leaves
  By Autumn breezes stirred.

And, as I wandered on and on,
  Close by the babbling brook,
And gazed the changing scenes upon,
  My thoughts in fancy took

Me back once more to bygone days,
  Those days of long ago;
And wrapt in mournful memories
  My heart o'erflowed with woe.

For there in fancy I could see
  The form I loved so well—
What blissful rambles there—Ah, me;
  What joys—I cannot tell.

But many years have passed away
  Since we walked side by side,
And I, who now am old and gray,
  Lament my long lost bride.

For in yon cold churchyard she sleeps
   Beneath the grassy mound,
Where oft I kneel and lonely weep
   Upon that sacred ground.

AN ODE TO AUTUMN.

SUMMER-TIME is ended,
   Harvest too is past;
Fruits and grain are gathered
   Safely in at last—
Hark! The song of gladness,
   Ringing loud and clear—
See! The swift wing'd swallows,
   Circling in the air,
For their flight preparing,
   To warmer regions bound—
Leaves in showers are falling
   Swiftly to the ground,
Toss'd by Autumn breezes,
   O'er the pathway strewn—
Evening gathers quickly,
   And the silvery moon
Rides along in splendour—
   Stars their lustre shed,
Like pure diamonds sparkling
   Twinkling overhead—
Chilling winds remind us
   Winter draweth near,
With its icy fetters,
   Binding on its bier.
All that now looks lovely,
   In its chilly arms,
Robbing beauteous nature
   Of her summer charms.
Thus each moving season
   Quickly hastes along.
Spring will follow Winter,
   Bringing its sweet song—

So, our lives are changing :
    Childhood first appears,
Youth and manhood follow,
    Then declining years.
Old age is the Winter,
    Wrinkling soon the brow—
Death doth quickly follow,
    Ending life below.
But the resurrection
    Brings new life again,
And in endless springtide
    Souls immortal reign.

WINTER.

WINTER MUSINGS.

WINTER again has come. The snow falls fast
And spreads its mantle over all the earth ;
The trees have shed their leaves and naked stand,
Bereft of autumn's garb. The birds of song
Are silent, not a note of music thrills
Our ears, while death-like stillness reigns around.
The sun has lost its bright and cheering rays,
And for a time all nature, wrapped in calm
Similitude of death, is held fast bound
By winter's icy grasp, as with a chain ;
Nor shall she wake again, or show a sign
Of animating life, till Springtide comes
And, with its resurrecting force, shall loose
Or break the bonds which bind her fast. Then will
The sun again shine forth o'er hill and dale,
And pour its genial warmth on all around,
While all creation shall with life renewed
Unite in one accord, to greet and praise
The Lord of earth and sky, Whose mighty hand

Controls, and keeps with unresisting power
The wheels of nature moving on.   Nor shall
The seasons, as they roll, fail or stand still,
But ceaseless move, until they each run out
Their destined course, and God Himself declares
That time on earth shall ever cease to be.

MISCELLANEOUS SONGS.

'TWAS IN THE MONTH OF MAY.

Oh ! 'twas in the month of May,
And my heart was light and gay,
As I took my sweetheart o'er the meadows green ;
Oh ! the daisies looked so sweet
As they bloomed beneath our feet,
And I wove them into garlands for my queen.

Oh ! the birds their songs were trilling !
And my heart, with love, was thrilling !
As we sat beneath the shady trysting tree—
Oh ! she promised to be mine,
And upon love's sacred shrine
Both our hands and hearts were joined so tenderly.

Oh ! 'twas in the month of June,
And the bells with merry tune
Filled the air with gladsome music, loud and clear—
Oh ! it was our wedding day,
And our hearts were blythe and gay,
As the village youths and maidens sang, *good cheer.*

FAREWELL, SWEET JESSIE.

Farewell, sweet Jessie, I must bid you good-bye,
　Though sad is the parting to me—
I leave you in sorrow, my fortune to try
　In a land far over the sea.

Oh !　Weep not, my darling, nor bid me to stay,
　Though my heart is breaking for thee ;
But pray for me, dearest, when I'm far away,
　In a land far over the sea.

And when I am toiling, my fortune to gain,
　Dear Jessie, my thoughts still shall be
Of the darling I left behind me in pain,
　When I sailed far over the sea.

But soon I'll return, love, with joy, and with pride,
　To share all my riches with thee ;
Then you, dearest Jessie, I'll claim for my bride,
　And no more roam over the sea.

ONCE UPON A TIME.

Once upon a time,
　　I knew a maiden fair,
　　And she had golden hair.
　Her eyes were violet blue,
　Her teeth were pearly white,
　Her heart was warm and true,
　Her steps were gay and light—
　　　That maid was my delight.

And once upon a time,
　　I woo'd that maiden fair
　　With bright and golden hair.
　I knelt down at her feet

And asked her to be mine ;
She said in accents sweet,
Her heart for me did pine—
          Nor could she then decline.

Then once upon a time,
          I wed that maiden fair,
          With soft and golden hair.
'Twas in the early spring,
When all was bright and gay,
The village bells did ring,
The folks made holiday,
          As I took my bride away.

But many years have pass'd,
          And she, who once was fair,
          With lovely golden hair,
Is now both old and grey.
For Winter's frost and snow
Have changed all to decay,
And silvered locks do now
          Bedeck her agèd brow.

And soon will come a time,
          When she with silvery hair,
          Who once was young and fair,
Will bid a fond good-bye.
And though we part in pain,
Yet, far beyond the sky,
We soon shall meet again
          In love's eternal reign.

DO NOT SAY "GOOD-BYE."

To say good-bye for aye, would give me pain—
     To thee, my love, I cannot say good-bye—
My heart would break, never to see again
     Thy lovely form. Then do not say, "Good-bye."

To say " good-bye," and never hear thy voice
　In merry laughter, rippling through the air ;
Nay, rather would I make " Grim Death " my choice
　Than never see again thy face so fair.

Then do not say "Good-bye " to me, for aye,
　But bid me cherish still my heart's desire—
That we may meet again.   And drive away
Dull care, and with new joy my life inspire.

Yet once again, my love, I now appeal—
　Yea, even on my bended knees, would try
That sentence to revoke—my joy to seal—
　Then say, " We'll meet again," and not "Good-bye."

MY SWEETHEART, MARIE.

I'LL sing of my sweetheart so joyous and gay,
She's fair as the flowers which blossom in May—
Her hair is like gold, and her eyes, bright and blue,
Her cheeks are as roses of delicate hue—
She's the queen of my heart, so happy and free,
She's the joy of my life, My Sweetheart, Marie.

Her steps like the fairy, are light as the air,
She skips o'er the meadows, so sprightly and fair ;
At the sound of her voice, all sorrow and pain
Doth vanish, as sunshine disperseth the rain.
She's the queen of my heart, so happy and free,
She's the joy of my life, My Sweetheart, Marie.

O soon may the time come, when her I can claim,
To be my companion, for no higher aim
Can I ever conceive, than to make her my bride,
And no greater bliss, than with her by my side ;
For she's queen of my heart, so happy and free,
She's the joy of my life, My Sweetheart, Marie.

MAGGIE.

OFT do I think of the days
 When we were young—Maggie—
When we joined in sweetest lays,
 That e'er were sung—Maggie—

I fancy I see thee now
 On the rustic seat—Maggie—
When first I pledged thee my vow,
 Mid our kisses sweet—Maggie—

And soon came the happy day
 When you and I—Maggie—
Were married and went away—
 Why do you sigh, Maggie ?

'Tis true, it is long ago—
 And now we are old—Maggie—
Winter with its storms and snow
 Its tale has told—Maggie—

But still we would not recall
 The days that are pass'd—Maggie—
Though night with its dark'ning pall
 Its shadows cast—Maggie—

For beyond the present life,
 So full of care—Maggie—
There is one, which, free from strife,
 We soon may share—Maggie—

Then wipe away all your tears,
 Let sadness be gone—Maggie—
Away with sorrow and fears—
 The battle's nigh won—Maggie.

QUEEN OF MY HEART.

QUEEN of my heart, love, for thee I am pining,
Oh, when shall I see thy sweet face again?
When shall my head on thy bosom reclining
Find sweetest repose from sorrow and pain?

By day and by night, love, waking or sleeping,
My thoughts are of thee—And oft in my dreams
I fancy I see thee—I wake! And with weeping
My pillow is bathed by sad gushing streams.

O could I but tell, love, where I might find thee,
Then nothing on earth should keep me away—
My arms in loving embraces would bind thee,
Nor should'st thou leave me in sorrow to stray.

But now my heart cries—Oh! Why didst thou leave me,
Alone in my sadness and anguish to pine?
Can it be true, did my soul so deceive me,
And must I for ever life's pleasures resign?

Is there no answer, must I, love, forget thee,
And blot from my heart thy memory so dear?
No more to think of the joy when I met thee,
And kissed thee so fondly, when no one was near?

Nay, I cannot forget thee, my dearest, my darling,
For my heart would nigh break, no more to behold
The face of my love, whose voice like the starling
So often hath cheered me in days of old.

Then fly to me, dear one, on love's swift wings sweeping,
O come to me now whatever betide;
For my eyes are dim with sorrow and weeping—
I wait for thy coming to make thee my bride.

Queen of my heart, love, for thee I am pining,
O when shall I see thy sweet face again?
When shall my head on thy bosom reclining
Find sweetest repose from sorrow and pain?

MY LOVE IS LIKE THE RED RED ROSE.

My love is like the red red rose,
The rose of early spring;
Her face with health and beauty glows—
And I her praise will sing.

Her steps are buoyant as the air—
Her laughter light and free;
No music is to me more rare—
No sweeter melody.

Her bonny eyes are sparkling bright,
Like gems of fairest hue—
She fills my soul with sweet delight,
And thrills me through and through.

Her ruby lips, with kisses sweet,
I fain would press to mine—
Her lithesome form so trim and neat
Fondly I would entwine.

YEARS MAY COME AND YEARS MAY GO.

Yes, years may come and years may go,
You may forget the past; but, oh,
I never can.   Those days gone by
Still linger in my memory.

And though in pain we now must part,
Yet still within my throbbing heart
No other love shall ever reign,
Though we may never meet again.

Your kindness I shall ne'er forget,
But often think when first we met
Beneath the shades of eventide,
And lovingly sat side by side.

Yes, there beneath the trysting tree
We sat, from care and sorrow free;
But now keen anguish tears my breast,
And robs me of my peace and rest.

O, could I hear thy voice again
In words of loving sweet refrain:
Recalling now that stern decree—
And bid me welcome back to thee.

Then would my heart, in sweet repose,
Find peace and rest from all my woes;
And on thy bosom safe recline,
Content to know that thou wert mine.

OLD ENGLAND FOR ME.

OLD England, the land of the brave and the free,
Wherever I roam, or wherever I be,
No spot in this wide world with thee can compare:
Who dwells 'neath thy banner, its freedom may share.
   Old England for me,
   Old England for me,
Is the song of my heart so happy and free.

The sun never sets over thy wide domain,
Thy sceptre is wielded o'er sea and o'er plain,
Nor can there be slaves where thy standard is seen—
Then here's to the health of my country and Queen.
   Old England, &c.

Then England for ever, the land of my birth—
I'll drink to thy bounty, mid pleasure and mirth;
And this is the song I will sing unto thee—
Old England for ever—Old England for me.
   Old England, &c.

FAREWELL.

Farewell, dear friend, we now must part—
Yet, oh! it wounds my aching heart,
To think that I no more may see
Your form divine—so fair to me—
Or ever hear your voice again
In loving songs of sweetest strain.

I never, never shall forget
The happy time when first we met—
How sweet the memory lingers still—
It often makes my bosom thrill
With joy that I cannot control—
A joy which bound us soul to soul.

But when I'm far away from thee,
Say, will you ever think of me?
Or will you very soon forget
That we together ever met?
And seek to crush beneath your feet
The memories of the past, so sweet?

Nay! Let us hope to meet again—
'Twould ease me of the throbbing pain
Which rends the vitals of my heart.
But, oh! to think that we may part
For aye! Alas! that it should be;
It fills my soul with misery.

THE OLD OAK TREE.

I sit beneath the old oak tree,
And fondly dream, my love, of thee—
Of happy days, when long ago,
Under its shades, the solemn vow
Was pledged, which nothing e'er can sever—
That vow which bound us one, for ever.

Near to this spot the silver stream
Runs, sparkling with the sun's bright beam,
And as it glides o'er pebbly bed
Reflects the blue sky overhead,
While visions sweet come gently stealing
Over my soul, love's bliss revealing.

Oh, that thou now wert by my side,
That I might claim thee for my bride.
Then would I with my arms entwine
In fond embrace thy form divine,
And through the sunny hours of day
Would pass the happy time away.

SONG.—SACRED.

I stood by the sea at midnight,
　　When the moon had risen high;
And its silvery light was streaming
　　Over the star-lit sky.

And I thought of the great Creator
　　Whose wisdom and power controls
The mighty expansive ocean
　　Which ever unceasing rolls.

And there, as I gazed with rapture
　　On the scene my eyes beheld,
My soul was o'erwhelmed with wonder,
　　And with joy my bosom swelled.

And this was the prayer I murmured:
　　" O Lord of earth, sky and sea,
" Be Thou my Guide and Defender,
　　" My hope through eternity."

UP IN THE MORNING EARLY.

Up in the morning early, my boys,
    Yes, up at the break of day—
" Tis the early bird that catches the worm "—
    Then up at the break of day.

" Early to bed, and early to rise "—
    This advice I give to you—
" 'Twill make you both healthy, wealthy and wise,"
    Is a saying old, yet true.

" Go to the ant, thou sluggard "—'tis said —
    " Consider her ways, and be wise "—
This is a lesson, quite easy to learn,
    A lesson you should not despise.

Then, " Don't let the grass grow under your feet"—
    But ever keep moving apace :
No laggard can ever expect to succeed
    In winning the goal in life's race.

The ladder of fame can only be climbed
    By those who are bold and true :
And, if you would reach ambition's fair height—
    You must rise with the morning dew.

CHORUS.

Up in the morning early, my boys,
    Yes, up at the break of day—
" 'Tis the early bird that catches the worm "—
    Then up at the break of day.

MY LOVE AND I.

My love and I sat side by side,
    Beneath the overhanging trees ;
Fast fell the shades of eventide—
    The leaves moved gently in the breeze.

'Twas there we pledged our solemn vow,
　The vow that did our hearts unite ;
I fancy I can see her now—
　The darling of my fond delight.

Her trembling hands were placed in mine,
　Her head fell gently on my breast :
I gazed upon her face divine,
　And knew that I her love possess'd.

Often since then my love and I
　Have sat beneath that shady bower,
And, wrapt in true felicity,
　Spent many a sweet and tranquil hour.

　　*　　　*　　　*　　　*　　　*

On the same seat, I once again
　Am sat in sadness, and alone—
My heart is full of grief and pain,
　For she, my love, is dead and gone.

NEVER MEET TROUBLE HALF-WAY.

To you who are harassed with sorrow
　These few words of advice, I pray
You will take—nor think of to-morrow—
　And never meet trouble half-way.

Our troubles are oft our own bringing,
　And sometimes engender despair ;
But, if we croaked less, and tried singing,
　They'd vanish away in thin air.

Now, what is the use of repining,
　And nursing the ills of our life ?
Or what do we gain by our whining?
　Will it help us in sorrow and strife ?

No, if we would banish our sadness
  And turn all our sorrow to joy,
If our hearts we would fill with gladness,
  And the cares of our life destroy,

We must always look out for the bright side;
  For there's many a cloudy day
That turns to sweet sunshine each noontide,
  And drives all the darkness away.

MY GUIDING STAR.

SACRED SONG.

My heart is filled with joy again—
  My drooping spirits lifted are—
Departed is my grief and pain,
  For I have found my *Guiding Star*.

Ere Thee I found, dark was my mind,
  And chaos did my soul possess ;
But now in Thee my Star I find,
  A light in this lone wilderness.

Shine on Thou Star of purest light,
  Nor ever hide Thy face from me—
For without Thee the dreary night
  Would almost endless seem to be.

Jesus, my Star, shine on, shine on
  Through all my path of life, and when
My journey ends the eternal Sun
  Shall guide me to the heavenly plain.

CHRISTMAS CAROLS, etc.

CHRISTMAS CAROL.

Shepherds o'er their flocks are keeping
  Midnight watch, while others sleeping
Know not that the time is near,
  When the long foretold Redeemer
Of mankind, the Lord and Saviour,
  Should in Bethlehem appear.

Suddenly upon them falling
  Comes a blaze of light appalling—
Brighter than the noon-day sun;
  Bending to the ground they tremble,
Filled with fear they close assemble,
  As they gaze the light upon.

Then with eager ears they listen,
  And with light their eyes do glisten,
As they hear a voice divine
  Saying, " Fear not, for I greet you—
"With glad tidings now I meet you,
  "And I give you for a sign :

" You shall find in Bethlehem's manger,
  " Wrapped in swaddling clothes, a Stranger,
" Who is Jesus Christ the Lord."
  Then a heavenly host appearing
Joined the chorus loud and cheering,
  Praising Him, with sweet accord.

CHRISTMAS BELLS.

Christmas bells again are ringing,
　Waits their carols sweetly singing
Join to greet the happy morn—
　Wake ye people, from your slumbers—
Wake ! and sing in tuneful numbers—
　Christ in Bethlehem is born.

Angel voices tell the story—
　Christ is born, the Lord of glory—
Shepherds listen to the strain—
　While they chant with holy pleasure
Joyful news, in happy measure—
　News that echoes o'er the plain.

See, the hosts of heaven appearing—
　Hark ! their voices sweet and cheering
Swell the chorus loud and clear—
　" Glory to the God of Heaven,
" Peace on earth to-day is given ;
　"Spread the tidings, far and near."

While the rapturous song is pealing
　Wise men from the East are kneeling
Round the Babe in Bethlehem.
　Earth and heaven combined rejoice,
Praising him with heart and voice—
　Crown Him with bright diadem.

CHRISTMAS CAROL.

ALL hail ! Redeemer, hail !
Saviour of all mankind,
Goodwill and peace on earth
In Him we all may find.

Join all the hosts above
In songs of joy and praise,
While we in anthems sweet
Our hearts and voices raise.

To shepherds it was told—
" Behold to you I bring
" Glad tidings of great joy ;
" A Saviour and a King

" Is born to you this day,
" And this shall be your sign :
" In Bethlehem's manger you
" Shall find the Babe Divine."

And then th' angelic choir
Took up the sweet refrain,
While earth re-echoed back
The wondrous joyful strain.

" Glory to God on high,
" Goodwill to all descend,
" And peace on earth be given,"
Saviour, Redeemer, Friend.

CHRISTMAS HYMN.

WAKE, ye Christians, from your slumbers
Rise to greet this happy morn,
Join to sing in tuneful numbers
Unto Him, Who once was born
In a manger poor and lowly—
Born a ruined world to save,
Born to make us pure and holy,
And redeem us from the grave.

Heavenly hosts on swift wings fleeting
Waft the tidings from above ;
Mortal tongues re-echo greeting
Joyful songs of peace and love ;
Let us chant the wondrous story
And with angels swell the strain,
" Christ the Saviour, Lord of Glory,
" World's Redeemer—born to reign."

CHRISTMAS BELLS ARE RINGING.

Christmas bells are ringing,
Joyful tidings bringing,
   Listen to the sound ;
Youth and age rejoice,
And, with heart and voice,
   Make the hills resound.

Angels' voices blending,
Heavenly hosts attending,
   Swell the chorus high ;
Peace on earth assuring,
Good-will e'er enduring,
   Echoes through the sky.

Shepherds tell the story,
Christ the Lord of Glory
   Comes to save mankind ;
Welcome, heavenly stranger,
Born in Bethlehem's manger,
   As a babe they find.

Christmas bells are ringing ;
We, our Carols singing,
   Hail the festive day ;
Saviour, we adore Thee,
Falling down before Thee,
   Chant our joyful lay.

NEW YEAR BELLS.

Ring in, ye bells, the glad New Year—
    Ding dong, ding dong—
With merry peals both loud and clear
    The strains prolong.

We hail with joy, with songs we greet
    This welcome day :
We worship at the Saviour's feet—
    And fervent pray

That every day, and every hour,
    Our lives may be
Guided by His Almighty power—
    From error free.

Oh, may His hand our footsteps guide
    In paths secure,
And may we never turn aside
    But firm endure.

That when on earth our lives shall cease
    We may be found
Where all is love and joy and peace,
    On heavenly ground.

, OUR LIVES ARE WANING.

Our lives are swiftly waning
And soon will pass away,
While all things now remaining
Will perish and decay.

O, whither are we tending?
What is our destiny?
Shall we, in bliss unending,
Dwell in Eternity?

Or shall we live for ever
In misery and woe?
Lord, grant that we may never
Into that darkness go.

May we at last inherit
In heaven's bright land above,
Through Christ our Saviour's merit,
Eternal peace and love.

———

Finis.

PRINTED BY S. COCKBURN AND SON,
THE BOROUGH WORKS AND "OBSERVER" OFFICE,
OSSETT.

www.ingramcontent.com/pod-product-compliance
Lightning Source LLC
Chambersburg PA
CBHW032110010726
47493CB00008B/2534

* 9 7 8 3 3 3 7 2 0 5 4 6 1 *